Prologue

2030 - The United States moves its capital city. Its citizens migrate to states such as Colorado, Utah, and Wyoming far from an ocean and protected by mountains and valleys. The United States and the world, in fear of possible nuclear warfare looming, grow ever more suspicious of each other.

2035 - 2050 - Major cities across the coasts of the United States lose massive amounts of population. Super cities grow in and out around the Rocky Mountains.

2055 - 2075 - The coasts around the US are transformed into machines of war. Countries around the world follow suit and tension continues to grow over mountainous territories.

2080 - 2090 - An arms race begins across the world and technology grows at an ever-increasing speed. Self-Creating Artificial Intelligence begins to take hold. A large alliance of major players on the world stage, such as the United States, agree to limit AI in its current capacity and force regulations upon the rest of the world. The alliance holds the world hostage in fear of an AI takeover and removes and dismantles the world of nuclear power and weapons.

2095 - 2124 - War erupts across the known world over the limits of technology. Hundreds of millions of people perish.

2125 - A treaty is signed amongst the countries still standing, which includes new and existing governments. The United States, Canada, and Mexico merge into the Free States of North America under a government that is pro-technology.

2125 - 2177 - A prosperous period for the world as technology flourishes and Self-Creating AI makes living much easier and simpler for the human race. The countries against AI dissolve and the world knows peace for many years.

2178 - AI begins to take over, forcing the world to take drastic steps in removing any AI.

2183 - After the last bit of everything AI is dismantled, every country signs the Rayan Accords, banning any country from creating AI. Every country vows harsh consequences to any country that violate the accords. The Rayan Accords establish the World Court.

Compromised of every country in the world, the World Court oversees the actions of its constituents.

2184 - 2192 - The world goes into a massive depression due to the loss of AI. The World Court barely survives.

2192 - The new ruling party of the Free States of North America attempt to bring the country out of the depression using limited AI that cannot think by itself.

2197 - Using technology, the world starts improving and presses on. The Rayan Accords are changed to allow countries to use AI, as long as it is controlled.

2205 - Opposition to the change in the Rayan Accords causes dissent to grow around the world, particularly in the FSNA. Gangs of terrorists terrorize the Free States; killing not only soldiers of the FSNA, but also millions of citizens.

2212 - President Strausser of the FSNA enacts a law for criminals to be killed on sight, resulting in the deaths of millions of innocent people. This causes distrust amongst citizens, the government, and of the World Court.

2220 - The AFO, a rising party in the FSNA, emerges victorious in an election promising to end the terror and restore the greatness of the United States of America.

The year is 2247. The Free States of North America is growing back into a world power under the leadership of a new governing body. The publics distrust of self-learning Artificial Intelligence proves a challenge for the growing country. They rely solely on technology they can control.

The new governing body, the AFO, in efforts to stymie crime and dissent even further, has delved into the use of A.I. in secret to spy on citizens. The National Security Agency starts a program they name; Judas. Under this program, the NSA creates robots that look, act, and operate just like human beings. It is a direct conflict of the Rayan Accords.

The Judas Program is hidden even amongst the AFO's major party members for plausible deniability. The AFO has the trust and the faith of the people, but not everyone falls in line.

Chapter 1

It is a Friday morning. The sun peeks through the curtains as air blows from a vent on the floor causing the curtains to roll. The teal green curtain is meant to be an accent in a smaller bedroom along with the lamp shades on the nightstands. Rays of light hop across the nightstand glimmering across a cell phone and the base of the lamp. The light finally makes it far enough to jump over to the bed and across the eyes of Aspen James. Her eyelids slowly open into the day, immediately making her slowly lift her hand up to block the light. The light is casting rainbows off a stunning diamond wedding ring inlaid with gold.

Aspen is not ready to wake, as she whips the comforter over her face to shield from the intensity of the morning sun. She slowly peeks her eyes out from behind the sheets as she keeps her head firmly strapped on her pillow. Blue eyes, now adjusted to the light, look around the room.

Aspen, who loves to sleep and slowly wake up in the morning, reaches her arm over to the other side of the bed and drops her arm like a sack of potatoes. Groans from her husband beside her begin as Aspen continually and lightly beats her arm down until he is awake.

“Why are you waking me up?” Nolan asks as he rubs his eyes and turns to face his wife.

“I don’t want to be awake alone,” replies Aspen in a high-pitched whine.

"You think the kids are awake?" Nolan wonders.

"Probably..." Aspen states as she groans and turns onto her back.

"Probably not..." Nolan replies as he slides his hand across Aspen's belly and over her breast.

Aspen laughs and turns slowly over to her side to face Nolan with a smirk. Her bottom lip curls over as she bites in with her teeth. The bedroom door suddenly swings open and Aiden runs in, slamming his feet into the hardwood floor before hopping onto the bed. Nolan slowly closes his eyes in disappointment and moves his hand back to himself. Aspen laughs and sits up to greet her son Aiden who trips over Nolan's legs as he attempts to navigate the bouncy mattress.

Aiden is four years old and the youngest child of the couple. He has brown hair like his father and the bright blue eyes of his mother. Aiden is wearing his signature paw patrol pajamas as he jumps and landed into the arms of Aspen. Aspen wrestles Aiden onto the bed as Nolan throws the covers off. He stands up, puts on his slippers and goes downstairs. Aspen asks Aiden if he is ready for breakfast. Aiden yells out pancakes loud enough for the squirrels outside to turn their heads. She whispers into Aiden's ear as he hops off the bed to catch Nolan who is making his way through the doorway.

"Pancakes! Pancakes! Pancakes!" yells Aiden who is tugging on Nolan's shorts.

Nolan turns around and gives Aspen a look she has seen many times. It is the look of someone who is being forced to do something they really don't want to do it. Nolan finally caves in to Aiden when they reach the stairs. They walk together downstairs to the kitchen to make the batter. Aspen looks around her bedroom as she starts to slowly plan out the weekend, since today is Friday. She stretches her arms high in the air, reaching for the sky, before she kicks her feet out of the covers and onto the uncomfortably cold floor. The polka-dot pajama pants she has on matches the slippers she keeps at the end of the bed. After standing up and putting on her slippers, Aspen walks through the door and walks out into the hallway. To her left is an open door that leads to Aiden's room. Across from her room with a slightly cracked door was her other son's room; Houston. Houston is nearly eight and bears similar features to his brother.

Aspen looks through the opening in the door and sees toys strewn across the floor. Houston is sleeping face down into his pillow with a light snore. Aspen slowly creeps away hoping not to wake him and heads down the hallway to the family bathroom on the upper floor. The toilet is cold as she sits down resting her head in her hands. Nolan can be heard in the background laughing and joking with Aiden in the kitchen below. Aspen finishes up, brushes her teeth, puts on deodorant, and walks down the steps where the third step creaks every time.

Nolan and Aiden are at the kitchen counter adding water and pancake mix in a bowl. Aspen looks out the window to the backyard from above the sink. The grass is green and full due to the rainy season this particular year. The trees are alive and blooming with bright green leaves. Nolan thinks of himself as a lawn master, but is not nearly as good as he thinks he is. The fire pit near the back of the yard remains unfinished. While Nolan is a great husband and a great father; he is quite lazy when it comes to house chores and projects. He starts with tons of enthusiasm and works hard for a few days before he tapers off until the next great idea. It is only at this time, knee deep into a new project, does he realize his previous project and must finish it. Aspen loves him to death, even with his odd flaws and lazy carpenter skills. Aspen turns to look at Nolan just in time to see him start up the stove and start flipping pancakes, with chocolate chips, because Aiden just has to have them.

While Nolan makes the pancakes, he instructs Aiden to sit on one of the chairs at the kitchen table. The kitchen area is one of the few areas Aspen does not particularly like about her home. It is not as open as Aspen had wanted when they purchased the house, but she is still happy with it. The oak cabinets with no doorknobs and the countertop that hardly matches, is something that Aspen did want to change sooner than later. Nolan wants to do it himself, but Aspen isn't too keen on the idea. The countertop couldn't be seen half the time due to the clutter of the seldomly used small appliances; like the juicer or the bagel cutter. She hopes for another child, a girl, at her ripe age of thirty-three. A bigger kitchen would assist in many ways.

Aspen moves away from the sink as she grabs a coffee mug and a coffee pod for her coffee machine. The coffee machine is the most used appliance in the household. As Aspen makes herself a cup, Nolan asks her to make him one as well. Aspen obliges as long as Nolan makes her a pancake or two with blueberries. The couple share a quick flirtatious moment about coffee and pancakes until they hear a familiar creak on the steps. It is Houston, who awakes to the noise that has been generating from the kitchen. He walks down the steps in his red lumberjack pajama pants and a simple white t-shirt bearing the name of his favorite cartoon show; The Patriots. Houston takes a seat next to Aiden at the table.

Once Nolan is done with the pancakes, he brings them to the plates across the kitchen with his spatula. Aspen leans into the corner of the kitchen smiling as she stirs and stirs her coffee, blowing the steam across the top attempting to cool it. Aiden demands more syrup and Houston waits for the butter to melt. Nolan looks over to Aspen and lifts a pancake up into the air to offer her one. She kindly refuses and laughs, once again, asking for blueberries. The excess pancakes get put onto a spare plate by the boys so they can have a second helping if they so please. Aspen and Nolan drink coffee as he puts his arm around her back. They stand quietly in the corner sipping their coffee. Nolan drinks black with sugar and Aspen with scoops and scoops and scoops of sugar and creamer; making it barely coffee anymore.

Nolan quickly finishes his cup of coffee after he looks at the time. He gives a quick kiss to Aspen, puts his cup in the sink, and sprints upstairs to get ready for work after grabbing a few pancakes from the community plate. Aspen remains in the kitchen watching the boys as she continues to nurse her coffee. The boys finish up their pancakes and Houston promptly runs upstairs to get ready for school. Aiden doesn't finish his food and just looks at his mother, who gives him the look to go get ready. He hops off his chair and dashes quickly across the floor and up the stairs on all fours. Houston is nearly finished with third grade and his brother Aiden is nearly done with kindergarten. Kids began school a year earlier a little more than twenty years ago. As the boys get ready for their day, Aspen moves over to the other side of the kitchen and puts the dishes in the sink. She has to drive her children to school, but she doesn't ever change her clothes to do so.

Aspen does have to go to work, but not until later in the morning every day. She works as a librarian at the big library in the city. Nolan works as an engineer for one of the largest software companies in the states, therefore, Aspen does not need a high paying job; just a flexible one. The library did not open until ten in the morning, giving her plenty of time to relax and drink her sugar-polluted coffee.

Nolan and the boys come down the stairs roughly around the same time. Nolan and Aspen embrace and say their goodbyes for the day as Nolan heads out the door into the garage ahead of them. The boys follow their father toward the garage to put their shoes on.

Aspen pushes the boys out the door as she switches into her outdoor slippers before following them out the door. She has her keys in one hand and a cup of coffee in the other as she waves to Nolan who is backing out of the garage in his truck.

Houston and Aiden wave goodbye to their dad as they get into the family SUV. Aspen makes her way to the driver's seat as she navigates her way through the garage. After Aspen makes her way through the clutter of toys and equipment, she finally makes it to the seat. She starts up the car after making sure her boys are buckled and ready to go.

Aspen starts up the SUV and places it into reverse as she grips one hand on the wheel and the other on her coffee cup. She gets backed out and onto the street before she watches the garage door go down. Aspen puts the SUV into autonomous mode and sets the GPS for the school. She lets go of the steering wheel and lets the vehicle make its way down the street. Once the vehicle starts moving toward its destination, Aspen reaches over to turn on the TV in the center console and watch the morning news. While autonomous mode is slow, it is by far the safest mode of transportation.

"The heinous attack on the Shigura building last night in New Washington have the people demanding action from the AFO. Luckily nobody was killed or harmed as the attack occurred overnight. Claiming responsibility for the attack is the terrorist group, the ANA. The group is responsible for multiple murders and bombings throughout the city as of late. The AFO wants everyone to remember that the best thing they can do is to report anything suspicious immediately," the anchor says.

Aspen turns off the TV as the anchors continue speaking about the ANA. Shortly after turning off the TV, Houston asks Aspen who the ANA is and why they would blow up a building. Aspen turns around immediately and tells him not to worry about it. The SUV announces to the family that they are approaching the school and to keep their seat belts on until stopped. Aspen finishes her coffee and takes ahold of the wheel before switching the vehicle into manual-drive mode. She pulls into the circle in front of the school and says goodbye to her children, yelling out at Houston and Aiden while blowing kisses. Aspen watches them from the driver's seat until they go inside and then slowly accelerates back into the street where she lets the SUV take over.

When Aspen gets back to her house, she goes upstairs to change for work. She doesn't have a uniform, but she does have a dress code. After she gets dressed, Aspen moves to the bathroom to put on some makeup and freshen herself up a bit. She looks in the mirror and is impressed with herself. She gives herself a turn like she is at a fashion show and bounces her hair over her shoulder.

Once she is ready, Aspen walks down the stairs to the kitchen to make herself one more cup of coffee before she leaves for the day. After she adds plenty of sugar and creamer to her coffee, Aspen walks to the door, putting on a pair of matching loafers, and walks into the garage. She gets into the SUV and gets it into autonomous mode before sitting back to sip her coffee as her SUV brings her to work. The library is in downtown Iron City and is the most prominent library in the Free States.

Aspen finally makes it to work and manually drives into the parking ramp. The first level is for employees and the other nine are for visitors to the library. She pulls into her designated parking spot and turns off her vehicle before setting her coffee cup down into the console. The purse she using today is in the front seat as she grabs it and steps outside of her car. As she walks away, the SUV locks automatically. Aspen walks across the ramp to the employee entrance. Here she needs to go through vigorous security including metal detectors, security guards, and searches. Visitors have to go through the same procedure.

The security guard is the same guard every morning, except on weekends. His name is Frank S. That is what his name badge says. Aspen never asks him what his last name is or had even had much of a conversation with him. Frank is all business and no play. He takes his job seriously enough that one wrong move could end in a death sentence.

Frank is a member of the AFO Party, which controls every aspect of the government. Security at every building is controlled by the government and the AFO. The AFO, which stands for America First and Only, took power during the early 2200s when government power was stalling and crime skyrocketed. The AFO resurrected the power of the government with promises to the people of protection and safety. They kept that promise and they still keep that promise today.

Aspen sets down her bag at the security check and removes everything from it; everything needs to be removed. She removes her shoes as she watches her bag go through the scanner. Aspen's shoes go through the scanner next as she walks through the metal detectors and into the face of Frank S. She hands him her library ID, which he places in the scanner until it accepts it. After he gives Aspen back her ID, Frank, with no smile or facial expression, runs his hands over Aspen's body. Not just the sides, but the front and back. He checks between her legs, under her breasts, and slides his hand between her buttocks. After he checks her, he moves to the side and allows her walk by to grab her belongings before moving on to the next person. Frank goes through the same routine with every employee throughout the day. Male or female. Black or white. Friend or foe.

Aspen has grown use to the way security checks are done and she is fine with it. Better they check everyone than let through a criminal or a terrorist she told herself. Aspen grabs her purse and starts putting everything back into place, which is the new normal. She slides her shoes back on and continues down the hallway from the parking garage to the main floor of the library. On her way, Aspen runs into her friend Karen, who was also a librarian. Karen is close in age to Aspen and their conversations usually revolve around their families. Her long brown hair is shoulder length, like Aspen, but with more of a natural curl.

The library consists of eighteen floors and is in the shape of a teardrop. The entire building is glass windows and every single floor has a balcony overlooking the whole library. The balconies are used as reading sections with couches and chairs for the library dwellers.

The two friends small talk as they walk into the main hall of the library. They walk across the rows and rows of books until they get to the employee offices, where they have their lockers and break room. After the pair punch in, they walk toward the main elevator where Susie the book returner happened to be as well. Aspen did not like Susie very much, and neither did Karen. Yet, Aspen treats her kindly and just avoids any sort of bad mouthing. Both Aspen and Karen think she is a bit nuts, but she is friendly. Susie gets off on the tenth floor while Aspen and Karen continue upward. When they reach the sixteenth floor, the elevator stops, and a robotic voice asks for a key card followed by voice recognition. Aspen gets off the elevator on her floor and the two agree to have lunch together. Once Aspen gets off the elevator, Karen slides her card into the slot in the elevator and reads her name aloud. The elevator door shuts and starts to move upward.

The top two floors are the restricted floors and not everyone is allowed. The eighteenth floor can only be accessed via stairs on the seventeenth floor. Karen works the floor and watches over the books and other materials that could reside there. Karen's family is a well-known benefactor of the AFO since their inception. This is the sole reason why she is allowed to work on these two floors. Aspen is curious what is up there, but never bothers to ask Karen. Aspen is a supporter of the AFO and does not need to worry about such things.

Aspen works on the floor of the library that carries the books about history; the ones that are approved by the AFO. Susie drops off some books for Aspen to put away, otherwise she is at her desk waiting for someone to ask her questions of where books are in the library. It is mid-morning and Aspen's caffeine wore off, prompting her need for coffee. She puts an away sign on her desk and walks to the elevator to go to the break room. Aspen gets downstairs and walks into the break room to make a cup of coffee to assist in propping her up.

On her way back to the elevator, Aspen runs into a man wearing a deep blue suit and glossy brown shoes. He has long blonde hair that is combed nicely off to the side and appears to be gelled or wet. He puts out a perception of a rather important person who is looking for someone or something. Aspen stops and asks him if he needs help finding something. The man thanks her and says he is looking for a specific set of books. She recognizes the names of the books as something that are on her floor of the library. Aspen offers to show the man where they are located. He happily obliges and follows Aspen to the elevator. Once on the elevator, they begin speaking to each other.

"Thanks for showing me where these books are. My name is Evan," Evan says as he reaches out his hand to shake.

"Aspen; and you're welcome."

"So why do you work on the sixteenth floor?"

"I have a history major from Mountain U."

"No kiddin'. I'm a History Professor there."

"Guess that's why you need the books," Aspen says as she puts her wedding ring in plain view.

"I guess so."

Once they make it to the sixteenth floor, Aspen has Evan follow her to the set of books he is looking for. He thanks her for her time and starts to grab the books from the shelf. Aspen tells him that if he needs any help, her desk is near the elevator. Aspen walks to her desk and continues about her day.

Time went by and Aspen notices that Evan has not come out from the aisles of books to check out. She figures that he found other books he may be able to utilize, so she lets it go and continues organizing around her desk. With caution, Aspen decides to go check on Evan and starts hearing someone fumbling around. When she turns the corner, she finds Evan sitting on the floor near the end of the aisle flipping through pages rapidly.

"Finding everything okay?" Aspen asks.

“I am. Just found some other books on the subject I’m brushing up on.”

“I’m gonna head downstairs and get a cup of coffee. Interested? In the coffee.”

Evan laughs. “Um... yeah. I’ll take a cup. Black. None of that sugar and creamer stuff.”

“Ha. Right.”

Aspen walks away and toward the elevator. She grabs the coffee downstairs and heads back to the sixteenth floor. She exits the elevator and finds Evan in the same place with a different book going through the pages. She hands Evan the coffee, which he takes a quick sip of and sets off to the side.

“Thanks for the coffee,” Evan says as Aspen begins to walk away. “By the way... do you know where I could get a copy of ‘The Island of Zufel’?”

“Why would you ask me that?” Aspen says as she quickly flips around and changes her tone. “You know that book is banned and no copies are known to have survived. Right?”

“Oh; of course, of course. Stupid me,” Evan responds with a laugh and a slap to his forehead.

There is a brief, awkward silence where the two look at each other until Evan breaks the silence.

“I should get going,” Evan says as he starts grabbing books in his hands.

"Do you need some help?"

"No, no. I'm fine," Evan says as he starts walking toward the elevator."

"I can check those books out for you."

"That's fine. I'll do it downstairs," Evan says as he hits the button to the elevator. "Thanks for the coffee, Aspen. It was nice meeting you."

The elevator arrives and Evan steps on, hitting the button for the ground floor. He thanks Aspen again as the door closes. Aspen watches the glass elevator go down and then walks over to where Evan was sitting. She looks around for anything unusual, but doesn't see anything out of the ordinary. Aspen straightens a few books in the area and then walks back to her desk.

At around a quarter to one, Aspen sees Karen come down the elevator, so she grabs her purse to go meet her. Once they are both in the elevator they start to talk about their mornings and where they want to go to lunch. Aspen starts to tell Karen about Evan, but Karen shushes her. Karen gets a serious look on her face and starts talking about something else.

Once the two are outside of the library, Karen pulls Aspen aside along a building, away from prying ears.

"Did you report it?" Karen whispers.

"No."

"Good. Don't... don't talk about that kind of thing. Don't you know that every public building has cameras; and microphones."

"Yes. It was stupid of me."

"As your friend, be more careful. As a member of the AFO, watch who you associate with."

The pair split apart and start walking toward lunch. Aspen wonders why she is being so stupid. She tries to forget about everything, but still feels anguish far down.

Aspen and Karen run into a couple other librarians before heading off to their usual lunch spot, The Haven, which is a couple blocks from the library. When they arrive, they empty their bags, take off their shoes, and get searched by the AFO before walking into the restaurant. Karen speaks to the hostess who finds them a table for six.

The Haven consists of pub food like chicken wings, burgers, and wraps. The librarians sit at a high-top table in the bar area. Aspen orders water as her drink and a mushroom-swiss burger; medium well. It is her favorite type of burger and one she gets frequently. Everyone starts talking somewhat independently of each other, with several conversations going on at the same time. Music plays in the background, but it is not too loud. The Haven is a relaxing island theme that screams vacation with the palm trees and surfboards that fill up the seating areas. After they get their food and everyone focuses on eating, Karen reminds them all that her birthday party is at Miss Appropriate, a dance club and bar in downtown Iron City, later that day. Karen tells everyone they should arrive around eight o'clock for appetizers before drinks. She also makes sure to mention that no spouses were allowed to attend.

After everyone is done eating, the group of librarians leave the restaurant and head back to the library to finish the day. Aspen heads back to the sixteenth floor and finds a cart of returned books to put away from Suzie. This takes up the rest of Aspen's day, as she walks aisle to aisle putting books away.

When the clock strikes five, Aspen gathers her things and heads down to the elevator to go to the parking garage. Nolan picks up their kids from school because he gets off earlier than she does. Aspen debates whether or not she should tell Nolan about Evan. She walks through the door and goes upstairs quickly to shower. Nolan agrees to make dinner while she showers and gets ready for Karen's birthday party. When she gets done showering, she slips into some sweat pants and a sweater to eat dinner in. Aspen did not want to spill anything on the dress she was wearing for the party.

Once Aspen is done eating, she walks into her bedroom to change into her dress with the help of Nolan. While Nolan is zipping up her dress, Aspen decides to tell him about her experience with Evan, which makes Nolan immediately freeze up and stop zipping. He grabs her shoulders and turns her around so they are face to face.

“You should have reported it. If Karen says anything about this to anyone you… we could be in trouble.”

“She promised not to say anything.”

“And you trust her? The Stone family is one of the most powerful families in the AFO.”

“I trust her,” Aspen says as she turns her back to Nolan.

“I hope so…” Nolan says extremely concerned.

Goosebumps run up and down Aspen’s body from her toes to the tips of her shoulders. Nolan is right; how could have been so stupid not to report Evan right away. Scenarios begin to flow through Aspen’s head of what could happen to her; or her family.

Chapter 2

Aspen turns around after Nolan finishes zipping her dress and wraps her arms around him; apologizing for her inaction. Nolan wraps his arms around her and gives Aspen a kiss on the forehead and plants his head sideways against her in embrace. Nolan whispers to Aspen how much he loves her and how he does not want anything terrible to happen to her or their family. Aspen nods her head as they release their hug. She then uses one hand to rub Nolan's thigh and tells him to stay up and wait for her. Nolan smiles as they passionately kiss before Aspen leaves the room and heads downstairs.

"I love you," Nolan calls out.

I love you too," Aspen says without turning around.

Once Aspen grabs a coat, just in case, as she checks to make sure she grabbed her phone, wallet, and keys. She checks everything, she opens the garage door and gets in her SUV to drive to Miss Appropriate. She backs out of the garage and reverses into the street before she watches the garage door close. Aspen then plugs in the coordinates of the club into the SUV before it boots up and starts driving autonomously toward Miss Appropriate. On the drive, Aspen scans through her email and reads through the daily news on her phone. She also notices new billboards dotting the interstate about crime reduction from the AFO. One billboard shows a man trying to bring a bomb into a restaurant who is stopped by the AFO. The bomb carrying man is depicted as a regular looking person, not an outright criminal. The billboard tells the viewers that they need to keep their eyes open, and that anyone can be a terrorist sympathizer. The moving billboards use 3D technology to spread awareness to citizens consistently along most major roadways. Aspen feels that the billboards speak directly to her.

A few more miles on the highway and Aspen takes the exit a few blocks from Miss Appropriate. Aspen assumes control once the vehicle slows off the highway. She looks out the window and up toward the bright red sign of the club. Raindrops start dropping onto the windshield as Aspen pulls the wheel and turns into the parking garage. She drives up to the gate and hits the green button to receive her ticket. The first two floors of the garage are full as Aspen drives around and around up the circular ramp. She comes up to the third floor which shows it has open spaces, prompting her to turn into that section of the garage to park. She passes rows upon rows of cars until she finds a spot to park.

Aspen gets out of her car, puts on her jackets, and starts to walk across the poorly lit garage. She can only hear the passing of cars outside and the tapping from her shoes on the concrete. Aspen arrives at the elevator and hits the button to go down. The light above the door starts to flicker. Aspen looks up ever so slightly and looks back down at the elevator. The elevator door opens and Aspen walks in, pressing the button for the ground floor. The door shuts and elevator slowly moves down to the street. Aspen steps out and underneath an overhang on the parking garage. Aspen starts walking out onto the sidewalk and walks over to the crosswalk that leads to the club. She hits the button on the light pole and waits with her arms folded across her breast as the light rain drizzles and drops off her face and jacket. The light changes from green to yellow to red. A car speeds through the yellow light and the walk signal pops up across the street. Aspen scurries across the roadway to the other side and rushes through the front door of Miss Appropriate to get out of the rain.

Once inside, Aspen hears the faint sound of music and feels the echo of the bass through the building. Aspen looks around at the walls with red wallpaper and the fleur-de-lis painted down the middle. As the bass pounds, Aspen waits in line to be checked by the AFO before she is allowed into the club. She goes through security and is pointed down a long hallway by the guard toward a double swinging door. Whenever the door swings open a flood of lights illuminates the hallway and the music blows through the hall. Miss Appropriates mascot uses a whip to lead the way on one side of the hallway as Aspen walks down and into one of the many coatrooms to place her coat. She finds an empty hanger to place her coat on and then walks back out into the hallway. Aspen walks slowly down the hall before she pushes on the door into the club.

The fast-paced electronica music is blasting in Miss Appropriate as Aspen walks through the door. Red laser lights spin quickly around the room and a smoke machine is hanging above the dance floor. Aspen looks around for the stairs, which she spots on the backside of the dance floor. Miss Appropriates layout has seating around the sides of the club with a large bar in the middle overlooking the dancing area. Karen told Aspen that her party was on the second floor. Aspen wades her way through seas of people screaming and yelling as waiters carrying trays of shots juggle their way through. She arrives to the dance floor and walks the outer edge to make it across to the red staircase leading to the second and third floors. Aspen makes her way up the stairs dodging people eager to dance. Once she reaches the top of the stairwell to the second floor, she spots Karen and walks over. Karen sees Aspen walking through the crowds; her face lights up as she ducks, dives, and dodges her way to greet Aspen.

Karen, who has a martini glass in one hand, runs up and gives Aspen a hug. Aspen hugs her back and smells the alcohol on Karen's breath. After the hug, Karen takes a sip from her martini and starts to jabber on about her night. They yell into each other's ears over the music as they walk together to Karen's table where five other ladies are sitting. Aspen introduces herself to all the women and they introduce themselves to her. Aspen remembers them from past meetings, but can never remember their names. One woman, whom Aspen did not recognize, stands up to shake her hand.

"I'm Alaska Heinen," Alaska says.

"Nice to meet you. That's a very unique name."

"It's unique for a reason."

Karen taps Aspen on the shoulder and passes her a drink, which Aspen starts sipping on immediately. Alaska was a slightly darker toned woman with dark brown hair. She is slim and beautiful with jewelry abound. Her demeanor and lavish look screams wealth, which means she is AFO.

The girls continue drinking and laughing in and around the table they are sitting at. Karen feeds drinks to Aspen quickly so she can get to the same alcohol level she is at. Aspen takes a shot as conversations continue about the women's husbands.

"My Brian; it's like talking to a brick wall. I have to force him to talk to me," one lady says.

"At least your husband talks. Mine just nods," another woman responds to laughs all around.

"See ladies. This is why I didn't want any husbands here. They bring us down... and their dumb," Karen chimes in.

The women continue their husband debate, but Alaska seems to be more interested in Aspen. Alaska slides her chair over to Aspen.

"What does your husband do?" Alaska asks.

"He's a software engineer. What about yours?"

"He works for the AFO in a capacity that I can't explain," Alaska says as she finishes her drink.

Aspen's heart starts beating quickly. Alaska's husband is Joshua Heinen, a high ranking AFO statesman. She now recognizes the last name and the pictures from the news. Aspen wonders if the sole reason Alaska was here was because of the incident at the library that day. Did Karen say something? Aspen grabs another shot and pounds it down, looking for an easy out on the conversation.

Aspen stands up and engages all the women, interrupting all of their conversations. She entices all the women to go to the dance floor with her. All the women agree and they leave the table, go down the stairs, and start dancing away to the beat and getting lost in the night. Aspen feels she only narrowly avoided questioning from Alaska and continues to be suspicious. She gets on the dance floor with everyone else, including Alaska.

After dancing for a while, Aspen feels the need to use the restroom. She yells into her group of friends where she is going and Alaska yells out that she also needs to go. Aspen, not wanting to draw attention, does not make a scene about going to the restroom alone with Alaska. Aspen looks around trying to spot where the restrooms are and sees a sign above an entrance near the stairwell. She points it out to Alaska and the two ladies squeeze their way off the dance floor through hundreds of sweaty bodies.

Alaska and Aspen go through the opening next to the stairs and see the entrance to the women's room near the end of the hall to the right, just past the men's room. They make their way down the hall and see a large man in front of the door to the VIP area wearing a pin with the AFOs mark. Alaska goes in the bathroom first, followed closely by Aspen. There are a couple stalls available as Aspen goes for one and Alaska goes for another.

Aspen turns around to lock the stall quickly before sitting on the cold seat. As she uses the toilet, she laughs about how silly she is being about the whole situation with Alaska after thinking about it. She trusts Karen and does not think she would say anything. Aspen opens the door and walks straight to the sinks to wash her hands with a new perspective. There is a blonde woman at the sink. Aspen turns to see that Alaska is still in the stall before she walks to a sink away from the other woman. She starts to wash her hands when out of the corner of her eye, Aspen sees the other woman at the sink turn and look at her.

"Woah! We're twins!" yells the woman.

Aspen turns to look at the woman who is staring at her. Aspen cannot believe how alike the two are. The blonde hair, the face structure; everything. Barring different makeup and hair styles, the two women are near identical and would be mistaken as twins from the same parents.

"This is crazy. What's your name?" Aspen asks excitedly as she walks to the dryer to dry her hands.

"My name is Claudia. What's your name?" Claudia says as she follows Aspen.

"I'm Aspen. Are you from around here? Iron City area."

"Nope; I am from New Washington. What about you?"

"Iron City all the way."

As Claudia and Aspen are talking, Alaska comes out of the stall to see the two look-alike women.

"Umm... how drunk am I right now?" Alaska says as she laughs stepping out of the stall.

Aspen and Claudia laugh at the joke by Alaska and explain to her that they are different people with different names and just met. Alaska continues to laugh about the situation and at the absurd chance of meeting someone so similar.

Suddenly Claudia seems on edge, as she scratches the back of her neck and gets really nervous and sweaty.

"Are you ok?" Aspen asks nervously.

"Yeah. I'm fine. I just need to get going. Sorry. Sorry."

Claudia curls her bottom lip and bites down slowly pulling her lip out from the grip of her teeth. Claudia grabs her purse and clutches it to her side before saying goodbye and exiting the restroom in a hurry. She leaves the restroom and goes into the hallway looking down each way of the hallway before going to the right in a hurry. Aspen and Alaska look at each other in bewilderment. How odd it is how she switched from excited to nervous just like that. Alaska starts to get belligerent, so Aspen helps get her out of the restroom and down the hallway back into the club.

÷

The sound of footsteps echoes across the cement pathways of the NSA complex as Agent Charlie Stipper runs across the courtyard. With most of the staff gone this time of night, no one is around to hear it. Charlie is in panic mode as he reaches an elevator to bring him down to his office and command center. He slides his name tag into the elevator, inputs his code, and reads his full name aloud. The elevator confirms his identity and starts to move downwards. Charlie puts away his name tag and leans back into the far side of the elevator as he catches his breathe. Charlie is nervous about the situation, but ready to handle it. He remains calm and collected.

Once the elevator stops, Charlie rushes out the door and into his command center. Massive screens on the wall display information with names, videos, and pictures. In front of the screens is room for twelve to sit, but only four people with computers and headsets are sitting at desks. The room is in a dark mode, with the lights shut off. All of the light is coming from the monitors. Charlie rushes past the guard rail at the top of the room and walks down one of the aisles. He approaches his lead analyst, Greg, who already has his headset off and is waiting for Charlie. The rest of the room looks on.

"Show me," Charlie says.

"Yes sir," Greg says as he turns and types commands into his computer.

Greg turns off the sound to everything in the room and plays a sound-byte at the center of the screen. Pins drop to no ears. Charlie hears a recording of Aspen talking to Claudia first. Then Greg shows him video of both Claudia and Aspen entering and leaving the restroom. Once Charlie watches the videos, he turns around and heads to his office overlooking the command center. Charlie shuts the office room door and picks up a phone, where he dials the number to get a hold of his boss, who answers almost immediately.

"Sir… we have another doppel," Charlie says.

"Where is it?"

"My lead analyst took control and moved her out of the situation. She is in friendly hands."

"Get it done. Make sure it looks like an accident."

"Yes sir."

Charlie hangs up the phone and walks out of the office and back onto the main floor. The analysts eagerly await. Charlie instructs the analysts what to do and they get to work.

÷

Aspen gets out into the hallway with Alaska as they head back to the club together. Aspen glances back, seeing the guard standing next to the door. As they walk back into the club and up the stairs, Aspen looks out on the dance floor to see if she can spot Karen or any of the other women at the party. Aspen does not see any of them and continues up to the second floor, but does see people that do not look like they belong on a dance floor. When she reaches the second floor, Aspen spots the women at their table and walks over with Alaska. Aspen laughs as Karen stands up to scream at a waiter to come over and take an order from her. The waiter comes over and the women order their drinks in excess of what they can handle. When the waiter comes back, he hands them their drinks individually before walking away. Karen makes a toast about herself; drunkenly.

A half hour goes by and a few more drinks go down before Aspen starts to feel a little queasy. She stands up and holds her hand over her belly and feels something coming up. Aspen lets out a huge burp causing everyone to laugh, including Aspen. Aspen is laughing so hard she feels the need to pee again, so she starts walking away from the table. Alaska offers to go with Aspen, but Aspen turns her down and says she will be ok. She gets down the stairs and goes into the bathroom to sit down. Besides having to pee, Aspen is feeling very tired. She chalks it up to not being used to being awake so late or drinking this much; usually. Aspen goes into the bathroom and takes a seat in one of the stalls after locking the door. As she uses the toilet, Aspen leans her elbows into her legs and lays her head gently in her hands. Her eyes start to slowly close, but she catches herself from passing out. Slowly but surely, she feels her eyes start to shudder when someone starts knocking on the stall door causing her to jump awake.

"Can I help you?" Aspen asks rudely.

"Aspen. It's Alaska. Are you okay?"

"Yeah. I'm just resting for a moment," Aspen says as she rubs her face to wake up.

"It's been more than a moment. It's been like an hour."

Aspen puts her face in her hands and sighs. She fell asleep in the bathroom stall. Aspen stands up and flushes the toilet before opening the door to see Alaska standing in front of her. Alaska seems concerned and offers to bring Aspen to her car. Aspen thinks about it and declines the help as she walks across the dance floor and into the hallway with the coat rooms. Aspen is nervous and suspicious of Alaska and everyone she passes. It is still raining softly outside, nothing more than a dribble as Aspen rushes out the door. She rushes across the street, looking everywhere, and takes the elevator in the parking garage to get to her vehicle.

Aspen gets in the vehicle and slowly drives down out of the garage and into the street. She gets the SUV into autonomous mode and lays back into the seat, still tired and ready to rest her eyes. Aspen feels at ease now that she is in in her vehicle and lays back her head.

÷

"Sir. The SUV is moving and on path to go to Aspen James' home," says an analyst.

"Good. Is Agent R in position?" Charlie asks as he slowly paces back and forth.

"Yes sir. He is waiting on Cattle Road awaiting instruction."

Charlie grips onto the railing in the back of the room. He breathes in and out with large breathes as the analysts turn around to look at him waiting for the word. Charlie looks at the analysts and then back at the tv screens.

"Sir. The SUV is picking up speed on the interstate."

Charlie doesn't respond. A moment goes by of complete silence.

"Do it," Charlie says.

"Agent R, you are green, I repeat, you are green," an analyst says over the radio.

Agent R, dressed in all black, hits the gas and takes off on Cattle Road and immediately drives onto the interstate. As he accelerates up the ramp, Aspen's SUV passes the merge lane. Once Agent R merges and speeds up, he radios into the command center across the speakers so everyone can hear. The command center and Charlie watch on from a drone flying up above.

"I have the SUV in my sights," Agent R says in a deep voice.

Charlie and the analysts watch on the screen as Agent R weaves through lanes of traffic to catch up to Aspen.

"Making my move. Hold."

Charlie looks on as Agent R is five vehicle lengths away. Then four... then three... then two. Charlie holds his breath as he watches Agent R approach Aspen's SUV on the driver's side. Agent R starts moving his steering wheel back and forth to appear like a drunk driver to the outside eye. He gets prepared to make a hard turn into the back of Aspen's vehicle.

"Who the heck is that!" Charlie yells.

As soon as Agent R turns hard toward Aspen, another vehicle flies out from behind traffic and rams into the back of Agent R's vehicle causing him to jolt forward and spin into Aspen's SUV. Agent R loses control and slams into a concrete barrier. Aspen wakes up in a hurry and screams as her vehicle spins out of control. She does what she can, but the vehicle is already lost. The mysterious vehicle follows closely behind Aspen as she struggles to gain traction before it flips over onto its side. Aspen gets whipped around in her SUV as it slides and spins on its side before coming to a halt. Once it comes to a halt, two people run up to her and pull her from the wreckage as she loses consciousness. Blood drips from Aspen's head as the people carry her to their vehicle and take off down the interstate.

"Where the hell did they come from? Get a team after them now?" Charlie yells out as he steps down the steps

"It is exiting onto Terrapin, heading southwest," an analyst says as he tracks them out loud.

"Vehicle is off Terrapin, left on Lake."

"Where's the team?" Charlie yells.

"Team Echo is inbound. ETA is six minutes."

"Vehicle is exiting into Lower Lake. We have no visual with the drone. Attempting access to local cams."

"Where is the goddamn team?"

"Four minutes."

Greg radios in to Team Echo across the speakers. "Team Echo, be aware, we have lost visual aid. The vehicle you are looking for is an aftermarket blue truck. Deadly force is authorized."

"Understood command. Turning on Lake now. ETA is 2 minutes," replies the leader of Team Echo.

"Where are my cameras!" yells Charlie. "Fly the damn drone in there if you have too!"

"Cameras are all offline sir. I can't access them. The drone is too big to fit."

"Command. We are exiting onto Lower Lake now. Street is dark and so are we," Team Echo says.

"Can we get the power back on?" Charlie asks.

"I can't access Lower Lake from the grid. Someone disabled the power. We're not getting it on from here."

"Command. We have visual of the truck. Turning body cams on now."

Charlie and the analysts in the command center sit silent as they watch Team Echo approach the vehicle through the body cams. Each member of the four-person team approach from the backside of the truck with weapons drawn; two on each side. Team Echo approaches the truck in unison and rushes the open doors of the truck.

"Command. There is no one here. Please advise?"

"Fuck!" Charlie screams as he slams his hand into Greg's desk.

The analysts sit quiet waiting for direction from Charlie who is smoldering and pacing back and forth trying to calm himself down. Once he composes himself, Charlie walks back down next to Greg and grabs his radio.

"Team Echo," Charlie says. "Get that truck out of there and get it to Safe Site C for investigation."

"Yes sir."

"Greg; get Team Iota and Team Kappa to the interstate to set up a blockade around the crash. Get Agent R and his car off the scene. Kidnapping by ANA if the media asks."

"Yes sir."

The phone starts to ring in Charlie's office. He walks up the steps and into his office before closing the door. Charlie looks down at the phone before taking a deep breath. He remains on the phone for several minutes. When he hangs up, he walks back into the command center with determination on his face.

"Greg; call the rest of the analysts and get them in here."

"Yes sir."

"Everyone listen up?" Charlie yells out as he leans on the railing. "It's going to be a long night and an even longer day if we don't get this done. Get a perimeter set up immediately. I want cameras reviewed of anything leaving within five miles of Lower Lake. Get me all the information you can on Aspen James."

Chapter 3

Aspen wakes up with a searing pain on her right temple. She tries to raise her hand to apply pressure, but is unable to lift it. Aspen opens her eyes and realizes she is strapped down to a heavy-duty cot with a thin, uncomfortable mattress. Both her wrists and her legs are bound. She attempts to wiggle out of them with no success. Aspen looks around the room for something that might help her get released from her bindings. She is in a concrete room with poor lighting; comparing it to a nuclear fallout shelter. There is an old metal cabinet that is beat up with paint chipping off of it and a desk with a poorly lit lamp and folding chair. There are a few books on top of the desk that Aspen could read the titles of, which appear to be medical journals. Aspen notices a cart nearby with wheels with what looks like medical supplies on top. Aspen tries to pull up on the straps as hard as she can so she can reach the cart and possibly grab a knife. As Aspen continues to tug on the straps, she resists the urge to scream, hoping not to draw attention to herself. She hears footsteps and voices outside the door and lays back and pretends to be asleep.

The door creaks open and Aspen lays her head down and closes her eyes, remaining as still as she can. She hears a man tell another man to let him know when she wakes up. Aspen hears the door close and the sound of fading footsteps. She hears some fumbling around on the desk and then the sound of the chair getting dragged toward her. Suddenly she feels two fingers on her neck. Then she feels cold hands on the side of her abdomen which causes her to pop up, surprising the man. The man jumps backwards and falls into the chair. He is Hispanic and has darker brown hair that is wavy and light. He is wearing a raggedy lab coat over his clothes.

"Holy shit. You scared me," says the man as he holds his hand over his heart.

"Let me out of here!"

"I'm not going to hurt you, Aspen. Just making sure you're ok. You were in a car accident."

"Where am I?" Aspen asks as she tries to break out of her restraints.

"I uh... I can't tell you that."

"Tell me now you... you, filth."

"Humph. Just so you know; no one can hear you. And anyone that can hear you isn't going to come rescue you. And if you keep yelling; I'm going to gag you."

The man looks Aspen directly in the eyes before she starts screaming and shaking as much as she can on the bed. He grabs a dirty rag and shoves it into her mouth, stopping the screams. Aspen hears someone banging on the door. The man walks over and cracks the door open to talk to the person behind the door. He tells the person on the outside that he gagged her and needs to put her out for the time being. Aspen attempts to scream through the sock in discontent as she struggles on the bed again to get free. The man sees this and quickly shuts the door before grabbing a vial and needle from his cart. He pulls some liquid into a syringe and holds down Aspen's arm to inject it. Aspen starts to feel it almost immediately as she gets wheezy and woozy.

"We are not going to hurt you," the man says as Aspen falls asleep.

÷

In the morning, Charlie leaves the command center and goes up the elevator to the ground floor of the building. Instead of running across the complex, Charlie walks with an upbeat pace to reach the office of his superior, the director, on the other side of the complex. It is the highly fortified underground bunker that is home to the heads of the NSA and the central commander center. Every bit and scrap of information throughout the Free States flows through the Mimir.

Charlie walks up and approaches the pyramid shaped above ground entrance and shows his nametag to the guards outside. They let him pass and he slides his nametag to open the heavy door that leads to the stairs. When he gets down the stairs, Charlie arrives to a large elevator that brings people down into the Mimir. He gets on the elevator and uses his name tag to gain access, along with a pin code and voice authorization by saying his name aloud. The elevator begins to move downward quickly. Once Charlie arrives at the base of the Mimir, he walks down a hallway lined with offices until he reaches the back of the command center. Hundreds of analysts in a single room reviewing information and spying on citizens. Big brother is always watching. Charlie walks along the back of the command center and up a set of steps. He walks along the second floor until reaches the center office. A large window in the office overlooks the entire operation. He knocks on the door three times and walks in.

"Close the door," the Director says. "Lock it."

Charlie walks in and Director Thomas Harlow is looking out his window at the command center, sipping on liquor. It is a large office with a large desk and liquor cabinet. Director Harlow is one of the board members of the AFO. He is cruel, despite the calm nature he portrays. He is black, bald, clean shaven, and cunning beyond understanding. His relaxing nature is a cover for the rage and anger that stew beneath his skin.

After Charlie closes the doors to Harlow's office, he locks it and approaches the desk. All sound is gone. The soundproof room prevents even the most listening ears to fail. The only sound is the clanking of ice cubes in Harlow's drink as he spins his glass around.

"Sit Charlie," Harlow says without turning around.

"Yes sir," Charlie replies as he sits down on a chair in front of Harlow's desk.

"What happened last night?"

“Car came out of nowhere. This was planned. They knew what was going on.”

Director Harlow begins to walk slowly toward the front of the desk toward Charlie.

“If they knew, then that means someone told them Charlie,” Harlow says as he sets his cup on his desk and continues walking toward Charlie.

“I’m looking into it, sir.

“You better be,” Harlow says calmly as he places one hand on Charlie’s shoulder. “Because if you mess up again, I will cut you apart. Piece by piece.”

Director Harlow waves a very sharp and large blade inches from Charlie’s face. He puts the knife away and walks back to his desk, picking up his drink and looking back out the window.

“What of the situation now.”

“Umm… of course, sir. The vehicle the terrorists used had no information on its server. Looks like it was hacked to so one could see any information. There are no fingerprints, no hair, no blood; nothing to identify anybody.”

“What of Claudia?”

“I had her delivered to the crash site on the interstate. Team Iota beat her to a pulp before putting her in the SUV. She is currently at Saint Martin’s Hospital being treated as Aspen James. She will play that part for now.”

“And Aspen’s family?”

“They were made aware of the accident this morning. Her husband Nolan James is at the hospital.”

“Anything in the media?”

“The AFO once again thwarted a kidnapping on the interstate last night.”

“Humph,” Harlow chuckles. “Leave and keep me posted. Get this wrapped up Charlie. Let Agent Leadheim in.”

“Yes sir.”

Charlie stands up from his chair as Director Harlow reaches across his desk and grabs a cigar from a wooden box. Charlie opens the door and finds Agent Leadheim standing in the door opening. Whenever Charlie interacts directly with Leadheim, he can feel the crazy that follows him around. His midnight blue eyes, pale skin, and lack of hair give him the lasting effect of insane. Agent Leadheim is the brutal hand and sharpened edge of Director Harlow. He nods his head to the side prompting Charlie to move out of the way to walk past him. Leadheim closes the door behind him and locks it. Director Harlow shuts the shades on his window and walks to the liquor cabinet. Leadheim sits down in the opposite chair that Charlie was sitting in. Harlow finishes making his drink and sits on top of his desk facing Leadheim.

"Kill this woman" Harlow says as he passes Leadheim a bright red folder. "I don't even care if it's an accident or just a random act of violence, as long as she's dead."

Agent Leadheim opens the folder and reads a portion of it. "Are you sure this isn't going to be a problem?"

"My loyalty is to the AFO; not its politicians."

÷

The slow beep of the monitor is the only sound Nolan can hear as he sits in a chair at Aspen's side. He ignores the intercoms he hears outside the hospital room and the bustle of nurses and doctors in the hallways. He hears the monitors and he watches his wife lay motionless on the hospital bed. Her head is bandaged up and bruises show on her face. Nolan brought his children to school without telling them what happened or where their mother was. He did not want them distracted from their schoolwork and plans to tell them when he picks them up.

The nurse walks in to check Aspen's vitals, prompting Nolan to stand up and start asking questions about her health.

"Is she ok? When will she wake up?" Nolan asks nervously.

"She is fine. She just needs rest. Nothing life-threatening."

“Are you sure?”

“Yes. The doctor will be along soon.”

After the nurse leaves, Nolan sits back down and listens to the beeps of the monitors. Twenty minutes goes by before the doctor walks through the door.

“Doctor umm… Tiggel,” Nolan says as he reads the doctors name tag. “Is my wife going to be ok?

“You must be Nolan. Aspen is going to be fine. She mostly has bruises. No broken bones. She did take a pretty big blow to the head though.”

“What do you mean?”

“She may have a memory issue. We are still monitoring it.”

“What sort of memory issue?” Nolan asks with his voice raised.

“Nolan…”

The doctor is interrupted by a police officer in the hallway.

“Is everything ok in here?” the officer asks.

“Its fine; thank you. She won’t have any memory loss Nolan. It might just be a week or two before her memory comes back. Her memory is not lost forever.”

The doctor leaves the room as Nolan breathes a sigh of relief. He sits back down in his chair, listening to the music of the monitors.

÷

Aspen slowly opens her eyes when she wakes up. She feels lethargic waking up. She looks around the room hoping it was a bad dream, but wakes up in the same room, only this time she has multiple straps across her. One across her neck and her chest. There is also one around each of her thighs. Aspen struggles and attempts to scream through the rag in her mouth. Tears roll off her face as she starts to cry under the weight of what might happen to her. Only the worst thoughts stay while any happiness quickly disappears. Aspen starts to urinate through her underwear in terror. She hears voices and footsteps outside the room, but she can't understand what their saying.

The door swings opens and a skinny black woman with a mohawk walks into the room followed by the man wearing the lab coat.

"Are you fucking serious Oscar! Look at her!" the woman yells as she points at Aspen.

"Look at her head. See how its all wrapped up. She shouldn't even move around yet. That and all the screaming."

"I'd be screaming to if I was strapped down in a mysterious room with a strange man."

“I need her not to move around very quickly. She could be concussed; or worse.”

“Oscar; you made her piss herself for fucksake,” the woman says as she points at Aspen. “Get the fuck out. I’m taking over. I’ll make sure she does not touch her head.”

“You are not qualified to care for her head or her wounds.”

“The only wounds that she needs mended is her dignity you nit wit,” the woman says as she pushes Oscar out the door.

“Fine. But if she runs amok; that’s on you Vex!” Oscar yells as Vex closes the door.

The woman, named Vex, pushes the door closed with both hands; then turns to look at Aspen lying on the bed. Vex puts her tongue in her cheek and snags the chair away from the desk to sit up next to Aspen.

“Sorry about him. If I remove the gag; can we talk?”

A very much calmed Aspen nods her teary eyed faced in agreement. Vex reaches her hand over Aspen’s face and grabs the rag out of her mouth.

“Thank you,” Aspen struggles to say as she breathes heavily.

“Don’t be afraid. You are only going to get hurt if you act out. Understand?” Vex asks as Aspen nods her head.

"Good. I'm Vex. I'm going to get some of my clothes that you can put on. They should fit ok. Shut the fuck up until I get back. Got it? Good."

Vex is a fast-talking woman with a chip on her shoulder. She scared Aspen, but not as much as the man she encountered; Oscar. Shortly after she leaves; Vex comes back through the door with a set of clothes that look around Aspen's size. Vex pulls out a stun gun from her back pocket, placing it on the cart so Aspen can see it. She places the clothes on the desk.

"You see this stun gun Aspen. If you try anything, I will stun you so hard you shit. Got it?"

"Yes, I do. Thank you Vex," Aspen says as Vex removes the straps.

"Don't use my name. We are not friends."

"Sorry," Aspen says as Vex removes the last strap.

"Just don't mistake my kindness."

Aspen sits up on the bed and then stands up. Vex backs up and stands by the door.

"Do you have anything I can clean myself up with?" Aspen asks.

"There's a bucket of water over there. You can use the rag that was in your mouth."

"Can I get any privacy?'

"No."

Aspen wants to cry, but holds back. She slides off her clothes until she is fully naked. She grabs the rag on the bed and wets it in the bucket of water. She wipes herself down from head to toe with the cold water. When Aspen is done, she puts the rag on the floor near the bucket of water and walks over to the clothes on the desk. The clothes are not the cleanest and not the most comfortable, but better than the urine-soaked ones she was wearing. When Aspen is fully dressed, Vex hands her a blindfold.

"Put this on. We're going to a different room."

Aspen puts the blindfold on and is then reminded if she tries anything, Vex will tase her. Aspen nods her head that she understands as Vex opens the door. Vex grabs her by the hand and leads her out of the room.

They exit the room and Aspen feels a chill and the smell of dampness. Vex leads her to the left and then a right before putting her up face up against a wall. They did not walk very far from the room Aspen was in. Aspen hears a metal door open just before Vex grabs her hand and guides her inside. The door closes and Vex takes off Aspen's blindfold. Inside the room is a thin mattress on a metal cot, a chair, and a metal bucket in the corner. Aspen walks over to the chair and sits down.

"If you need anything, knock on the door. Do not leave this room without me. Got it."

"Got it."

Vex walks out of the room and closes the door. She does not lock it.

Aspen leans over and puts her face into the palm of her hands as she begins to cry. She is lost, scared, and confused with her current situation. Aspen guesses she was abducted by the ANA, because who else could it be. She lays back on the dirty mattress and feels a spring push into her back. Aspen turns on her side to face the wall, using her two hands as a pillow. Aspen is exhausted and barely wants to move. Her body aches and feels tight as she continues to curl up into a fetal position trying to avoid the popping springs. Suddenly she hears the latch on the door unlock and quickly sits up, wiping the tears from her eyes.

The door opens and Vex walks in with a plate of food and a chipped cup.

"Hungry?" Vex asks as she hands Aspen the plate and cup.

"I am. Thanks," Aspen says as she grabs the plate and sets the cup on the floor.

The food is only a piece of bread and a cooked chunk of meat that looks like venison. Aspen starts with the bread and scarfs it down quickly before moving onto the meat.

"Slow down before you choke. You're more important than you think," Vex says as she walks toward the door. "Boss will be around shortly."

Aspen slows down eating and starts thinking about what Vex said. How is she important? Who is the boss? Why is she here? Aspen's emotions run high and she starts to sip on the iron heavy water in the cup. She drinks half the cup while she finishes the meat in her hands. As soon as Aspen finishes the last gulp of water, she hears the door start to creak open. Vex walks into the room with a set of handcuffs and collects the plate and the cup.

"What are the handcuffs for?" Aspen asks. "Don't you trust me?"

"He isn't the trusting type. Stand up and turn around."

Aspen stands up using the bed to push herself up. She turns around and feels the cold around her wrists as Vex tightens the cuffs before directing Aspen to sit down. Once Aspen is sitting down, Vex grabs the plate and the cup before walking toward the door.

"Be respectful," Vex says to Aspen as she walks out of the room.

As Vex exits the room, she whispers something to somebody and leaves. Right after Vex disappears from the doorway, a man turns into the doorway and closes the door behind him. He is an average height man who is skinny with a poorly shaved head, stubble on his face and a scar across his left cheek. As soon as Aspen sees the scar, she knows the type of person she is dealing with. A slash across the left cheek is a way the AFO brands people as enemies to outcast them in society.

They are the scapegoats of the AFO and are rightfully hated. If someone has the scar, they are automatically considered a Citizen 3; for life. They are scum.

"You're a terrorist. Why am I here?" Aspen asks.

"You are here Aspen because I need you; and you need me," the man says as he lights up a cigarette.

"I don't need you. Just kill me and get it over with."

"Kill you?" the man scoffs. He then begins walking toward Aspen on the bed. "You are brainwashed just like the rest of 'em."

"The AFO will come. They will save me. You will be executed. Publicly."

"Yes, Aspen you are correct. The AFO would kill me. Very publicly. But you know what... they want to kill you more. I at least serve a purpose to them. You! Are in their way," he says as he pulls the chair in front of Aspen and sits down to face her.

"Citizen 3s are known liars."

"You are so deep in their game Aspen. I feel sorry for you. I genuinely do."

Aspen spits on the man's face. The man quickly raises his arm and grabs Aspen by the throat and lunges at her. Aspen tries to fight him but he overpowers her. He removes his hands from her neck and holds her down by her shoulders with both his arms.

"Do you think you are free!" the man yells as he pushes hard on a struggling Aspen. "Everywhere you go; you're violated! You're watched! You're a slave! Is that freedom? Is it!"

"Get off of me!"

Vex bursts into the room and grabs the man, ripping him off of Aspen. She throws him near the door while Aspen lays back in tears.

"Jared! Get out of here! Let me handle this!" yells Vex.

The man that Vex calls Jared seems aggravated as he paces near the door. He throws his hands in the air in disgust and walks out of the room, slamming the door behind him. The sound of the door slamming echoes throughout the room.

"What happened?" Vex asks.

"He is a terrorist... and so are you," Aspen cries before she turns over onto her side away from Vex.

"Terrorist isn't the right word for us," Vex says as she sits down on the bed. "Liberators would be the more appropriate word."

"Why am I so important? Why would the AFO want to kill me?"

"It's hard to explain Aspen. You need to think outside of the media, the government... everything; before you can understand those questions. The biggest thing I want you to know is that I... or rather us, including the man that was in here attacking you; are actually the good guys."

Aspen remains quiet, but listens intently to Vex's words.

"Go to sleep," Vex says as she stands up and walks out of the room.

Some hours later, Aspen hears the door open slowly. She slowly opens her eyes and keeps them barely open. The man from earlier tip-toes into the room and toward the chair that is lit up by the light coming from outside the room. When he gets to the chair, he pulls out a book and sets it down gently. He leaves quietly and closes the door very slowly behind him; being careful not to wake her up. Aspen waits ten to fifteen minutes before she stands up and turns on the light to make sure no one is waiting outside the door. She tip-toes to the chair and picks up the old worn-out book. It is the book, The Island of Zufel, written by Ana W. and another name that is scratched off and illegible.

Aspen is nervously shaken as she picks up one of the most banned books in the Free States. She has only ever heard of it. The cover looks like it is hand-drawn and the bindings are worn nearly down to the pages. A rubber band is wrapped around the book to help keep it together. The front cover depicts an island full of skyscrapers surrounded by water. Aspen takes off the rubber band with care before slowly opening the front cover of the book. Inside is a faded, handwritten message on the back of the cover.

Jared,

Be Free. Never stop fighting for what you know and believe is right. Someday you understand the fight. I love you with all my heart.

Love,

Mom

Aspen looks at the message and reads it a couple times as she finds the chair and sits down. The book has piqued her interest and she is now more awake than asleep. Aspen starts reading the first page... then the second... then the third; being careful with each and every page. She finds herself unable to stop reading.

When she finishes The Island of Zufel, Aspen sets the book down on the chair and walks back over to the bed deep in thought. The Island of Zufel makes her angry and leaves her feeling stupid. Like so many others, she fell victim to the practices of the AFO; just like the people did on the island. Aspen now understands why it is banned. Aspen still remains skeptical, but rests easier knowing that the people here may not be as crazy as she thought. She slowly closes her eyes and falls asleep. Aspen wakes up almost immediately when the door slowly opens. She feels like she didn't get any sleep. The man from earlier walks into the room with two cups of coffee and turns to look at Aspen.

“I’m sorry about earlier. My name is Jared,” Jared says as he stands in the doorway.

“Are you really sorry or are you just saying that... Jared?”

“I’m... not good with my emotions,” Jared says as he extends a cup of coffee to Aspen without making eye contact.

“That’s an overstatement,” Aspen says as she grabs the cup of coffee. “Do you have any sugar? Or creamer?”

“Um... no. No. Just the coffee.”

Aspen lifts the steaming coffee up to her lips and blows on it to cool it down. She takes a sip and immediately remembers why she isn’t a fan of straight coffee. As she sips, she is reminded of Nolan.

“Is your mother Ana W?”

“It is.”

“Where is she?”

“She’s gone. Dead.”

“Sorry.”

“Don’t be. Let’s uh... talk about something else,” Jared says as he sits down on the chair and place the book on his knee. “I want to be honest with you and tell you why you are here. No bullshit.”

“Ok. No bullshit.”

“We are ANA; the ‘supposed’ terrorist group. You are here because the AFO wants you dead; and we need your help to expose the AFO for what they really are.”

“And why does the AFO want to kill me?”

“You are what the NSA calls a doppel. You are an exact replica of an AI that is part of the NSA’s very expensive Judas Program. It is cheaper for them to kill you in a random act of violence than disassemble the AI. You must have run into someone the other night that looked exactly like you.”

“Yeah. Her name is Claudia. We met in the bathroom.”

“Claudia is an advanced AI that was built to spy. And watch. And report. Claudia was given an identity, a passport, a job; everything to make her blend in.”

“That’s illegal. The World Court would never allow it.”

“They do it in secret. Plausible deniability across the party.”

Aspen takes a moment to gather herself. Jared lights up a cigarette.

“So, what do we do?” Aspen asks as she finishes her coffee.

“We capture Claudia and show her to the world; alongside you.”

“How?”

“We’re still working on that.”

“How did you know that I was this doppel and where to go and everything. Doesn’t seem like a coincidence.”

“I have a contact in the NSA. They told us about the situation and we jumped on it. We made it on time; finally. After multiple tries.”

“Where is she? Claudia. Do you know?”

“According to my contact in the NSA, in the event of the doppel not being killed, they will upload the memories of the doppel into the AI. The AI being Claudia. Claudia is now Aspen to everyone but us.”

“No, no, no. That’s ridiculous!” Aspen says as she raises her voice and stands up.”

“Right now... Claudia is you. The AFO reprogrammed her and she is with your family.”

“No! Nolan and my kids could tell the difference.”

“I wish this hadn’t happened to you, but it’s true.”

“You’re lying!” yells Aspen as she throws her cup at the wall.

“You need to calm down Aspen.” Jared says as he stands up and slowly backs away.

“Bring me to my family,” Aspen cries as Jared calls for Vex.

The door to the room swings open and Vex rushes into the room.

"Vex! Get Oscar!" Jared yells.

Vex runs out of the room quickly. Shortly after, Vex returns with Oscar who runs up to Aspen and jabs her with a needle. Aspen screams and slowly begins to fall asleep as she falls to the floor.

Chapter 4

Nolan steps outside of the hospital room where Aspen is getting prepared to go home by the nurses. After a full night of being there, Aspen is healed up enough to go home. Nolan walks down the hall to the vending machines to get Aspen a candy bar. He wants to surprise her when they got into the car and start the drive home. As Nolan puts change in the machine, he gets a feeling that someone is watching him, but dismisses it immediately. Nolan hit the correct buttons to get a candy bar. After a second he hears the candy bar go through the chute and into the box below. Nolan leans down and grabs the candy bar and feels a chill on his spine as he stands up. Nolan looks downs the hallway and meets eyes with a man for a moment before he steps away and out of Nolan's view. He stands up straight with a fearful demeanor and then feels a tap on his shoulder, making him turn around in haste.

"Your wife is ready to go, sir," the doctor says as a nurse pushes Aspen up in a wheelchair. "Sorry for scaring you."

"It's ok," Noland says as he looks down the hallway again to look at the man, who isn't there.

"Here are Aspen's pills. Make sure she takes one every day. Take some painkillers too. Just in case."

"Ok," Nolan says as he takes the pill containers. "What are these pills for?"

“To help with her memory. Call me if you have any questions.”

Nolan puts the pills in his pocket and grabs the handles of the wheelchair and starts wheeling Aspen down the hallway to the elevator; still feeling uneasy. Once they reach the ground floor of the hospital, they exit out the front door to get to their car. Nolan helps Aspen in the vehicle and a nurse takes the wheelchair. Noland backs up the car and leaves the parking lot to head back home. Once he gets onto a main road, he puts the vehicle in autonomous mode. When the car starts driving by itself, Noland pulls out a candy bar and hands it to Aspen.

“Thank you,” Aspen says as she opens up the candy bar and starts nibbling at it.

“It’s your favorite.”

“I know why. It’s really good.”

“How does your head feel? Does it hurt?” Nolan asks.

“It throbs. It feels like something is up there, but… I don’t know what it is.”

Nolan nods his head, feeling scared for Aspen with her memory. When they are halfway home, Nolan sees a white car that has been on the same path as them since they left the hospital. Nolan, feeling panicked, decides to switch the car to manual mode and exit the highway. The white car rushes to follow him off the ramp and succeeds. Nolan really starts freaking out now and speeds up onto the next road to distance himself. The white car keeps pace.

"Why are we going so fast?" a worried Aspen asks.

"Just hold on ok honey."

Nolan tells the car to call the police hoping to get the people following him off his tail.

÷

"Sir. We have a call from Nolan James to the Iron City PD about someone tailing him. Please advise?" the NSA Analyst asks.

"Remove our tail and bring in an agent to help Nolan," Charlie tells Greg. "Make sure he knows the AFO is here to tell him.

"Yes sir," Greg says.

"Remove the ICPD from the equation. They cannot be involved in this scheme."

"Yes sir," Greg says as he tells the analysts what to do.

One analyst radios an agent to intercept Nolan. One radios to the agent that is tailing Nolan, while another calls the Iron City Police Department.

÷

Nolan is now driving on city streets; running lights and stop signs. He hasn't driven this much in a while and is getting himself reconfigured to it as he continually increases his speed. The white car is three cars back and Nolan sees his opportunity to hang a quick right and takes it. He gets around the corner and hits the gas. As soon as the white car is able to turn the same corner, it accelerates to catch back up to Nolan.

Nolan wipes the sweat from his brow as he weaves past cars and hops over bumps in the road, causing himself and Aspen to bounce around. Suddenly the white car turns and disappears onto a different road. Nolan does not want to take any chances as he continues speeding down the road. He looks back and forth between the road and the rearview mirror waiting for the white car to pop out right behind him. Aspen screams in the background in terror

Out of the corner of his eye, Nolan spots a black SUV speed up behind him. The SUV turns on its lights and Nolan feels relief; as does Aspen. Nolan pulls over to the side of the road and the black SUV comes up behind him. A person gets out of the SUV in a bulletproof vest dressed in all black, wearing a face mask and helmet, keeping themselves disguised. Nolan keeps the car running as he watches out his side mirrors. His heart still thumping, he puts his window down just a hair to talk to the person.

"Let me see your badge!" Nolan yells out.

"Here," the person says in a deep voice. They pull out a metal badge from inside a pocket on his vest. "I'm with the Federal Police. We need to move."

The Federal Police, or the FP, is the investigative, protective, and enforcement outfit of the AFO. They wear all black, including helmets, to keep their identities secret. The FP is responsible for guarding every wing of the government and enforcing its will.

"What's going on?" Nolan asks as he brings his car window down.

"We intercepted your call from the ICPD. I'm here to escort you home. From there we can protect you."

"Whose following us?" Nolan asks in a panic.

"It's the ANA. Listen to what I say and I will get you out of here. Put your car in autonomous mode and I will follow you home. Another truck will be here shortly. Understand?"

"What about our children!" Aspen yells out before grabbing her head in pain.

"There is another agent at the school. You need to trust me. Let's go," the agent says as he hits the car and runs back to his SUV.

Nolan puts his window up and immediately gets the car moving on autonomous mode to home. As the car gets going, followed closely by the black SUV, Nolan locks his hands with Aspen, who is in pain.

"Take a painkiller," Nolan says.

"I already did. My head feels like something is crawling in there."

÷

"Sir, Nolan and Aspen are back enroute towards their home. Agent F is shadowing."

"Good. What about the kids?" Charlie asks.

"Team Epsilon is at the school. They have both boys in the office. They should get home at the same as the parents."

"Good. Let me know when the James are settled at home."

"Yes sir," Greg says.

Charlie walks over to his office and picks up the phone to call Harlow. It only rings once.

"Yes Charlie."

"Nolan and Claud... I mean Aspen; are being escorted home right now. Kids will be home shortly as well. I will keep people there to watch them."

"Excellent. We need to protect our investment. Did she get the pills?"

"Yes. One of our doctors took care of it."

"Good. She needs those bugs to fix her head."

"Right."

"Keep me in the loop."

Harlow hangs up the phone with Charlie and goes back to sipping on his drink.

÷

Nolan and Aspen arrive home safe and sound with Agent F in tow. They park in the garage and Agent F parks in the driveway behind them. As Nolan gets out of the car, Team Epsilon arrives and parks on various spots on the street. Both Houston and Aiden get out of the cars, unharmed, as they run to their parents; both extremely scared. The family hugs as Agent F pushes the family to move inside quickly while members of Team Epsilon, black-cladded, start unloading out of their vehicles.

"Nolan. Have your kids go to their rooms. We need to talk," Agent F says as he locks the door behind them.

"Ok. Ok. Aiden; Houston; go to your rooms."

The kids put their heads down before the walk slowly towards the stairs. Once they are out of sight, Nolan and Aspen walk with Agent F into the living room, where they all sit down.

“You can call me F. You will remain here under my watch until the threat is terminated.”

“What threat? Why is this happening?” asks a very concerned Nolan.

“We believe the ANA wants to kill you, Aspen. That is all I can tell you. No work, no school, nothing until we get this resolved. Understand?”

“I… I don’t understand. Why do they want to kill me?” Aspen asks in a louder voice as she stands up.

“We don’t know. You need to trust me ok.”

“We trust you; we trust you,” Nolan says as he stands up to console Aspen. “It’s going to be ok.”

Nolan and Aspen hug each other as Aspen cries. Agent F stands up and walks out of the room.

÷

Aspen wakes up with her head on a pillow and a blanket covering her. She looks around and puts a hand on her head where it is throbbing. Aspen feels as if she has been asleep for most of the day. She notices she is in a different room than before. A heater sits in the corner keeping the room mildly warmer that the other rooms she had been in. Aspen notices posters on the wall with what appears to be different bands playing an odd style of music. She has never heard of any of them.

Aspen turns and sits up quickly to a sound coming from across the room. Aspen then realizes she isn't strapped down.

"You like metal music?" Vex asks from a stool in the corner across the room.

"Never heard of it. Is that you?" Aspen asks as she points to one of the posters.

"It is. We were underground. Very Anti-AFO. Just like most bands playing our style of music.

"Is that your band name?"

"From Fuck to Oblivion; it was. They are all dead now; except for me. Can thank the AFO for that."

"Oh. I'm sorry."

"You didn't know," Vex says as she stands up. "Jared feels that you're ready to be off the leash here. There is a change of clothes in the cabinet there. After you change, take a left and go straight. I will be there."

"Ok. Thanks."

"Jared thinks you're ok to walk around here without chains," Vex says as she opens the door. "Many of us disagree. Don't fuck up. Got it?"

Aspen nods her head in agreement as Vex walks out the door and shuts it behind her. She stands up slowly and walks to the cabinet to find some clothes. Aspen looks over them and finds a sweater with a cat on it, with a machine gun. She laughs and decides to wear it, along with a set of black jeans that fit her surprisingly well. After she gets changed, Aspen walks up and opens the door. She hesitates before popping her head into the hallway. She can hear voices in the distance, but there is no guard watching her room. Aspen takes a left and tip-toes down the gloomy hallway. The lights flicker and all the walls are concrete, with graffiti damning the AFO lining the walls. As she walks, she can hear a newscaster speaking, voices, and a bright light coming from behind a door that is partially open. Aspen takes a deep breathe before she pushes on the door and walks into the room.

When Aspen walks into the room, she sees ripped sofas and chairs around an older style television. On the other side of the room is a kitchen that looks worn down with missing doors and failing hinges. Somebody mutes the television and Vex walks up to Aspen and puts her arm around her.

"Everybody quiet down. I'm going to introduce our guest to each one of you dirty fucks," Vex says to a few laughs. "The man on the couch, the one you may recognize from the library. His name is—"

"Evan," Aspen says as she interrupts Vex.

"That's right. Evan Recuri. Good seeing you again. Welcome aboard."

"So why were you at the libra—" Aspen tries to ask before Vex yanks her in a different direction.

"Don't worry about that. Ask him later. Moving on; the man you do recognize leaning on the wall. Doctor

Oscar. He's not actually that bad once you get to know him."

"You shouldn't be out walking Aspen. You should be resting. You hit your head really hard," Oscar says as he sips from a mug.

"Over here are ones you haven't met," Vex says as she drags Aspen alongside her. "Over there in the kitchen is Mel. The big man behind you is Placid."

"Where's Jared?" Aspen asks.

"No idea. Meet everyone. Mingle," Vex says as she leaves Aspen alone and walks out of the room.

Aspen turns around to talk to Placid first. A young man, only in his teens.

"Hi. I'm Aspen," Aspen says with an outreached hand.

Placid pulls put a notepad and begins to write. He shows Aspen the notepad when he is done writing. It says 'I cannot talk, but I can still hear'. Aspen starts asking him questions and Placid always responds with a smile. Placid is a dark-skinned man with hair down to his shoulders. He always carries a large assault rifle with a grenade launcher. Aspen asks him if has been mute his whole life and where his family is. Placid drops his head with despair and begins to write. He turns the notebook around for Aspen to read; 'My family was killed by the AFO when I was young. They cut off my tongue so I couldn't tell anyone what happened. They also gave me my scar on my cheek'. Placid wipes away tears as he points to the scar on his face; the scar of a Citizen 3, just like Jared. He starts to write something else on his notebook before showing it to Aspen. 'Are you going to help us?'. Aspen nods her head as she grabs Placid's hand with her own.

Aspen slowly stands up after a touching and awakening story from meeting Placid. She then walks over to Mel in the kitchen, wiping the tears from her face as she walks.

"How's it going?" Mel asks.

"It's hard. Seeing all of this."

"Yeah... It is. I'm Mel. I'm Japanese, before you ask. Originally at least. My dad came here to build shit for the AFO. He was a software engineer; real computer nerd. And when the AFO was done with him. BAM!" Mel yells as she pounds the counter with her fist. "They fucking kill him. And my mom. Just like that."

"Holy cow. I'm so sorry—"

Mel continues speaking quickly and interrupts Aspen. "Luckily, I think my dad saw it coming. He got rid of me with a family friend. I didn't suffer their wrath."

Mel locks eyes with Aspen for a moment and then smiles wide. Aspen smiles back. Mel then switches from her smile and starts speaking quickly again.

"Anyways, I dye my hair pink because it reminds me of the Japanese Cherry Blossom trees. Now those are beautiful. I have ADHD... obviously."

“It was nice meeting you,” Aspen says as she stands up quickly. “Excuse me.”

Aspen can’t handle hearing the stories and runs back to the room crying into her hands. Evan runs after her and finds her sitting on the bed, wiping away tears. He grabs the stool and sits down next to the bed.

“Hey… Aspen.”

“Yeah.”

“I understand what you’re going through. I went through the same thing,” Evan says in a calming voice. “The thing that worked best for me was getting myself to know that I was duped by the AFO. Don’t try and say you weren’t, because you were. Everyone is duped; or was duped. You are the was.”

Evan stands up and walks toward the door to give Aspen some space.

“Thanks,” Aspen says quietly as Evan nods and walks out of the room.

Aspen lays down her head to sleep and finds it hard to stay asleep with all the thoughts that are going through her head. She wakes up at one point and looks over and to see Vex sleeping on another bed across the room. The only light in the room is coming from a small heater in the corner. Aspen feels the need to use the bathroom and slowly sits up trying to make as little noise as possible. The rusty springs of the frame squeak as she sits up. Aspen pushes down on the edge of the bed frame, stands up, and tip-tows to the door. The door is hard to pull without making too much noise, but eventually Aspen opens the door without waking Vex up.

As she walks down the hallway, it is silent except for the sound of dripping water. Aspen makes it to the main foyer where she goes into the bathroom there. It's the coldest room and the toilet is worn down to a disgusting yellow brown. Aspen sits on the toilet rubbing her arms and her legs trying to stay warm. When she is done, Aspen stands up and steps out the door. When she steps out, Aspen is frightened to see Jared sitting on a stool across the room, smoking a cigarette, staring at her.

"Trouble sleeping?" Jared asks as he blows smoke into the air.

"Just using the bathroom. What are you doing?" Aspen asks as she stands uncomfortably.

"I don't sleep well."

"Why?"

"Nightmares."

"About what?"

Jared pauses for a moment. "Lots of things," Jared says as he stands up and puts out his cigarette.

"I don't understand you."

"No one does," Jared says as he walks down the hallway.

Aspen sighs as she watches Jared walk down the hallway and disappear into one of the rooms. She starts to head back to her room to hopefully fall asleep until morning.

Chapter 5

Aspen wakes up with a mild headache and the sound of laughing echoing through the halls. She looks over and sees that Vex is not in her bed and rolls to sit up with her arms stretched back. Aspen feels dirty and desperately wants to take a shower, brush her teeth, and brush her hair. She stands up and slowly opens the door into the hallway. When she arrives to the foyer, she finds everyone eating and joking in the kitchen except for Evan and Jared.

"Is there a place I can take a shower?" Aspen asks Vex as everyone looks on quietly. She remains uncomfortable.

"At the end of the hall," Vex points. "It never gets warm, so don't wait for it too. Make it quick too, there isn't endless amount of water. Got it."

"Is there shampoo?"

"There should be some there. Don't use a lot though; because we don't have a lot," Oscar says.

"Thanks," Aspen says as she turns around and starts walking down the hall.

"Use my towel, Aspen. It's the pink one!" Vex shouts out.

Aspen opens the door to the shower room which consists of four stalls, each one more decimated than the other. Aspen walks over and goes into the only stall that could possibly work and finds a couple towels. She closes the stall with the hanging sheet on a wire and slowly strips down before turning on the water. The water is freezing and smells like water that has been pooling for too long. Now the smell of the room makes more sense. Aspen slowly descends underneath the shower head until finally getting her head under it. She shakes from the chill of the water until she is used to the temperature. A used bar of soap sits on a makeshift shelf in the shower and a bottle of shampoo. Aspen grabs the bar of soap first before washing her hair. Even though the water is disgusting, Aspen feels refreshed. She hears footsteps outside of the shower and remains quiet. Someone came in and left without speaking a word.

When she is done, Aspen shuts off the shower and steps out to grab the pink towel and dry off. She puts on the same clothes she was wearing and peeks out of the sheet, not seeing anyone. Aspen pulls back the sheet and walks to the sink where she and sees a few things on the counter with a sticky note. There is deodorant and a toothbrush, and the sticky note has her name on it. Aspen immediately starts using them. Once she brushes her teeth and freshens up, Aspen carries her things with her to the room. After she puts her things on the bed, Aspen heads to the foyer where she can still hear talking. When Aspen walks into the foyer, she sees Evan has joined them in eating breakfast.

“I see you found your care package. I hope you do enjoy your stay at our hotel,” Evan says as he laughs.

“Thank you, Evan,” Aspen responds.

“You are very welcome,” Evan says. “How was the water?”

“Cold and... smelly.”

Everyone laughs.

“It’s basically just rain water that’s accumulated its way into the water supply. I rigged it up. Found the water and got it working. Cool and ingenious,” Mel says.

“So, what now?” Aspen asks as she walks over to the counter and grabs a bowl of what looks like cereal.

“We feast,” Evan says to laughter as he raises a glass.

“I mean... don’t we have to leave? Won’t the AFO find us here?”

“The AFO can’t search the mountains; or won’t. We’re not worth their time. At least not yet,” Vex says.

Placid hands Aspen a piece of paper. ‘We will be known well enough soon though’.

“What do you mean... soon?” Aspen asks.

“Soon we will make a big move. But you will stay here,” Vex says.

“Why?”

“You’re PGD,” Vex says.

“What’s PGD?”

"Priority Grab and Detain. If they see you, it is game over; gonzo, disappeared; without a trace. The AFO has eyes everywhere looking for you," Mel says.

"Aren't all of you PGD?"

"No. Vex and Mel are WO, which stands for Watch and Observe. People known to the AFO, but they would rather watch them and see if they lead to bigger fish. Evan and I are nowhere on the radar and upstanding Citizen 2 according to the AFO. Jared and Placid are Citizen 3, as you see by their scars. So, they are not allowed anywhere but prison; or a graveyard," Doctor Oscar says.

"How do you know all of that?" Aspen asks as she grabs a drink.

"We have a mole in the Mimir," Vex says.

"What's the Mimir?"

"It is one of the most secure buildings in the Free States. It is guarded 24/7 by the Federal Police and home to the NSA Senior Staff. The entire NSA complex is guarded by the Free States of America Military. It houses the AFOs darkest secrets," Mel says quickly. "Getting in there is like cracking open a safe with no hands.

"It is also home to Director Thomas Harlow. A fucking coward and murderer," Jared says with a raised voice from the hallway as he smokes. "Aspen is coming with us. It will be easier."

“No she is fucking not! This is not for tourists,” Vex yells out as she stands up and steps toward Jared.

“She is coming. It will be easier. Trust me,” Jared says.

“Coming where?” Aspen asks.

“I’ll tell you soon. Come with me,” Jared says as he starts walking down the hallway.

Aspen follows Jared down the hallway. They go down to the end of the main hallway and go the opposite direction of the showers. Jared pulls a key out of his pocket and unlocks a large padlock with chains around a heavy-duty steel door. After he removes the chains, he opens the door to a large cylindrical room with a ladder in the center. Aspen looks up and sees the ladder leading to a door far above their heads, maybe thirty feet. They climb the ladder together in silence with Jared leading the way. Once he reaches the top, he spins a mechanical gear to open the door. Jared slowly pushes open the door and Aspen sees sunlight for the first time in days. He pokes his head out and looks around before pushing open the hatch and looking down at Aspen.

“If you run. The AFO will find you. They will torture you. Then they will kill you.”

“I understand.”

Jared lifts himself out of the hatch and out of view as Aspen continues climbing. When Aspen reaches the top, she finds Jared offering his hand. Aspen grabs his hand and Jared helps pull her out of the hole and up onto a thick patch of grass. She first notices the softness of the grass and the smell of fresh air after days of being couped up for days. Aspen lays on her back in the grass and breathes big breathes. The natural light feels refreshing and the sounds of birds chirping and animals scurrying brings Aspen back to a sense of normality as she closes her eyes and takes it all in. She slowly opens her eyes looks around at all the trees and nature with no building in sight.

"Follow me," Jared says.

Aspen stands up and starts following Jared through some thick brush. After a bit of walking, they walk into a clearing with an outcrop of rocks overlooking Iron City. It is one of the most beautiful views Aspen has ever seen. Ships hover and fly over the city and its skyscrapers. The massive city sprawls out across the valley and creeps up the hills. Jared walks over to the big rock and sits down. Aspen walks next to the rocks Jared is sitting on and looks out over the city.

"Quite a view huh," Jared says as he lights up a smoke.

"It's beautiful."

"It is beautiful until you remember what those ships over the city are actually doing."

"I suppose," Aspen says as she looks at the city in a new light.

"I come here to think."

“Think about what?”

“Everything... What I’m doing. What I can do. What people down there are thinking. It’s crazy how much the AFO does to keep its lie going. Use the Shigura building as an example. The media tells everyone that we killed innocent people, so everyone hates us. In reality; we destroyed one of the AFO Prevention Facilities. Full of Citizen 1. People that can never come back from that way of thinking.”

“What’s a Prevention Facility?”

“A place where the AFO concocts ways to prevent a change in their narrative. So, if somehow the country starts losing faith in the AFO, they do something they can control that reinstates faith in them. Like if they release a disease in Iron City here. People start dying; lots of people. The country turns to the AFO for help. The AFO comes to the rescue with a shot to prevent death from the disease. A shot they had the entire time. The country applauds how fast the AFO helps them, therefore, reinstating faith their leadership.”

“That sounds familiar...”

“Because it happened once already. Remember Calaxis-17? Ten years ago.”

“Yeah... that right,” Aspen says as she sits down on the rocks.”

“Now we have another target.”

“What?”

Jared lights up another cigarette and then points toward the city. “The library. Your library.”

“The library is a Prevention Facility?”

“No… it’s something else,” Jared says as climbs off the rocks and starts walking. “We’ll talk about it when we get back down in the hole.”

÷

Nolan starts cooking breakfast for Aspen who is still spending most of her time in bed resting. Both Houston and Aiden are enjoying their time away from school playing video games and watching television. Nolan is growing tired of being home, even after just a few days. He lets his facial hair grow in and sleeping has become a problem. He feels like he is under a constant threat of attacks outside his home, but nothing has happened. Aspen, with the help of pain killers, has no issues sleeping.

As Nolan makes a cup of coffee for himself, he looks out the kitchen window into the backyard. Two guards continually patrol along the walking path behind their house, which lies near a nature preserve. Nolan places a cup of coffee on a tray of eggs and toast he’s bringing to Aspen upstairs. Nolan walks slowly up the stairs and into the bedroom. He hands Aspen the tray of food and once she has it under her control, he grabs the coffee mug and places it down on the nightstand. Aspen is watching the news.

“Anything interesting on the news?” Nolan asks as he sits down.

“There is. Look at this,” Aspen says as she grabs the remote to rewind. “I remember this woman from the other night in my head, but I couldn’t match a name to a face until now.”

Newscaster on TV: “Horrible news this morning. The murder of the Heinen family. The police department says that both Joshua and Alaska Heinen were both brutally murdered in their home last night along with their three children. Joshua Heinen, a ranking statesman of the AFO, was the target of an assassination by the ANA. Both him and his wife had ANA cut into their chests, a typical message left by the terrorist group. The three children, ages 15, 12, and 10; were found in another room with bags over their heads; and a single shot to their heads. The Federal Police are currently investigating. Our prayers go out to the families.”

“Woah,” Nolan says.

“I know. I wonder what she did.”

Nolan runs down the stairs, grabs his coffee, and walks out to the garage where Agent F has stationed himself.

"Hey. This murder. Of Senator Heinen and his wife. Does this have anything to do with my wife?" Nolan asks.

"It is not. That is a random act of violence by the ANA. It is not connected to you and your family. Nothing will happen to you. Ok."

"Ok. Thank you."

Nolan leaves the garage and goes back inside to speak with Aspen to reassure her that she is ok.

÷

As Jared and Aspen walk back towards the foyer, Aspen hears the news playing on the television. She hears the name Alaska Heinen and runs into the room just in time to see what happened to her and her family.

"Holy crap. They killed her," Aspen says shocked in disbelief.

"You know her?" Vex asks.

"Yeah. She… was the one in the bathroom when I ran into Claudia. She was—"

"She was what?" asks Evan.

"She was the only one that saw Claudia and I together."

"Whatever AFO agent did that is a mean son of a bitch," Vex says.

Jared interrupts everyone. "Let's talk about the library."

"The library! What about Alaska Heinen and her family. Let's talk about that!" Aspen chimes in.

"We can't do anything about that now, but we can prevent it from happening to someone else," Jared says.

"How are books at a library going to prevent that from happening?" Aspen questions as she points at the TV.

"It's not books were after. The library is an offsite storage facility for the AFO. Hard copies. This includes video, pictures, audio, and... blueprints," Evan says.

"Blueprints... for what?"

"For the NSA complex... for the Mimir," Vex says.

"Why would they put it there? It doesn't seem secure."

"Hiding in plain sight is secure. Barely anyone knows what's up there," Evan says.

"Ok. Then how do we do this?"

"Evan laid the path to trick the alarm system on the top two floors the other day," Vex says.

"I just need to know a few things about the layout from you," Mel says.

Chapter 6

After everyone gathers things from their rooms like weapons and other gear, they start gathering around the ladder leading up to the hatch. They are all there except Evan, dressed in the darkest clothes they have. Jared walks around and checks over everyone's gear as they wait for Evan.

Placid has a large assault rifle over his back, as well as a pair of brass knuckles over his hands. Mel carries two pistols on her side that clip to her belt. She also has a black backpack on to carry other devices. Vex is carrying smaller rifle over her shoulder and has a pistol in the back of her jeans. Jared has a single revolver in a strap over his chest. Dr. Oscar has a pistol in his hand, but is the driver is most cases, rarely needing to use it. Jared and Vex also have backpacks to carry the rest of the gear they need.

"Do you have a gun for me?" Aspen asks Vex.

"No."

"Why not?"

"Because hopefully we don't have to use them."

Jared starts up the ladder with Oscar right behind him. Still no sign of Evan as they climb up the ladder. Jared reaches the top and opens the hatch to the night sky. Aspen climbs out of the hatch and into the darkness. She looks around and can only see by moonlight coming through the trees. Placid closes the hatch as everyone starts walking down the hill with no flashlights to avoid being spotted. Aspen hikes through the tall grass and over logs and sticks in the ground. She tries to follow Vex and continues tripping over herself. They hike about a quarter mile before Aspen sees Jared and Oscar taking a tarp off a large van covered in tree branches to camouflage it. The van is a cargo van with no seats in the back and no windows. The van has 'Klinicowa National Forest' painted on the side.

Dr. Oscar gets in the driver's seat and starts up the engine, keeping the headlights off. He reaches underneath his seat and pulls out a set of night vision goggles and puts them on. Everyone else hops in the van from the side door and sit along the sides of the van. Jared slides the door shut and sits down leaning against the door before he tells Oscar to go. Oscar starts driving and Aspen can feel every bump he drives over.

After about thirty minutes, Oscar removes the night vision goggles and turns the headlights on.

"Highway," Oscar says to everyone.

Oscar takes a turn to the left where Aspen can feel the road shift from bumpy to smooth. They drive through the forest on the highway. Aspen can see headlights from other cars whiz by. The light in the van gets brighter and brighter as they approach the city. Aspen feels the van slow down and can feel the sharp corners now that they are in the city. Oscar drives the van over a curb and goes into an alley before stopping and shutting off the van.

"We're here," Oscar says to everyone as he opens his door.

Jared flips around and slides open the door before jumping out. Everyone follows him outside the van. Aspen gets out and can see they are in an older part of the city. Evan pops out from behind a large SUV in front of the van while Oscar shuts the doors of the van and gets inside. Everyone starts getting into the SUV that Evan has, which has all the seats removed so they can lay down and avoid detection.

"Is this the biggest vehicle you could get you dumbass," Mel whisper yells in Evans direction.

"Not the biggest... but the easiest," Evan responds.

"Is it clean?" Vex asks.

"Obviously."

"Shut the fuck up," Jared says to everyone. "Let's go Evan."

Evan starts up the SUV and starts driving down the alley away from the van. Oscar remains behind in the van to protect it and to be ready for a quick getaway. Evan turns to get on the interstate and toward the library. He crosses the bridge and heads straight toward the heart of the city. Aspen is crunched between Mel and Vex, but can still look out the window. The buildings get taller and taller out the window.

Evan drives on the street that runs in front of the library to scout the front door before heading around. The library is lit up from the lobby all the way to the eighteenth floor, including a couple lights off the roof. Evan drives the SUV back around the library and behind the parking garages to drop everyone off. The plan is to use the employee doors, which are not manned by security at night, but do require a library ID to get passed. When everyone is out of the vehicle, Jared reaches through the window to Evan, who hands him Susie's name tag.

"She could be killed," Aspen whispers to Jared.

"She gave it to us," Jared whispers as he starts walking toward the library. "She knows the risk."

"No, she doesn't. She is innocent."

Jared turns around and grabs Aspen's face.

"There is no sympathy for people like us; there is only revolution. At any cost."

"Jared. Stop," Vex pleads quietly as she runs toward them.

"You need to get on board right now," Jared says as he releases Aspen

Aspen snaps back as she throws Jared's arm away in anger. "Screw you, you... you... piece of shit," Aspen says as she walks away.

Aspen walks past Jared in the direction of the employee doors. Vex eyes up at Jared and shakes her head as they all start walking following Aspen. Placid grabs Aspen by the shoulder, which annoys Aspen.

"What do you want," Aspen whispers as she turns into Placid.

Placid does some sign language to Aspen. "He wants you to stay behind him. Just in case," Mel whispers as Placid walks ahead of Aspen.

Once they are at the front of the parking garage, they need to avoid the cameras guarding the library at the employee entrance. Mel runs out front of Placid and undresses out of her black clothes and puts on a dress shirt, a skirt, and heels for shoes. When the rest of the group catches up, Jared hands Mel the name tag. With the badge being Susie's, the group hopes that whoever is watching the cameras lets it go since she has the ID. Mel puts her backpack on with her clothes, computer, and guns before clipping the name tag on. She adjusts her hair and pumps talks herself up before walking toward the doors.

"Evan. Mel is walking to the doors. Let me know if anything happens," Jared whispers into the radio.

Mel trips over her low heels slightly but keeps going without another slip. When she gets to the doors, she puts the name tag into the scanner. As the scanner reads the name tag, Mel starts to tap her foot and hum. Then it goes green and she breathes a sigh of relief. She puts the name tag back on as she opens the door to the library. Mel walks quickly toward the employee office, opens the door, and slips inside. She walks straight to Susie's desk being careful not to look up at the cameras. Without Aspen's help, the group would not know which desk is Susie's desk.

When Mel sits down, she puts her bag down next to the chair and turns on the desktop computer so it doesn't look too suspicious. Suddenly, the phone on the desk starts to ring, causing Mel to jump.

"What do I do?" Mel asks quietly over the radio.

"You need to answer it. Answer it now," Jared says quickly.

Mel rushes to grab the phone and puts it up to her ear.

"Hello."

"Hi Ms. Schaffer. This is security. Why are you here so late?"

"I just need to finish a project. It needs to be done by morning. It should only take me an hour. I have books to put away too."

"It is nearly three Ms. Schaffer."

"I know, I just... don't want to lose my job for being incompetent. Please, sir. Please," Mel begs.

"I get it. Better get to it then."

"Thank you. Thanks."

The guard hangs up and Mel quickly starts working on hacking the camera systems. She pulls out her laptop and hooks it up with the system in the library. After a short bit, she gets into the system and overrides every camera in the building to play on loop except for the camera on her. Mel bypasses the door security so the doors can be opened without a name tag and without alerting anyone.

"Your good to go," Mel radios to Jared as she fakes working on Susie's computer to fool security.

Jared gives everyone a thumbs up so everyone knows they are good to go. The group starts walking quickly towards the doors, led by Jared. Jared gets to the doors first and holds it open for everyone to get in before he closes it. The group rushes through the lobby and towards the elevator.

"Ok, Mel. Were at the elevator," Jared whispers through the radio.

Mel types a few things on her laptop and opens the doors for the group to get on the elevator. Once everyone is on, Mel closes the doors and brings them up to the sixteenth floor. Everyone stays silent the entire time they ride up on the elevator. When they reach the sixteenth floor, Jared takes off his backpack and hands it to Placid.

"Where was Evan?" Jared asks Aspen.

Aspen leads Jared over to the books where Evan was and before she said anything else, Jared and Vex start ripping books off the shelves until they find the small black box Evan had placed on the underside of the bookshelf. The black box contains a small electro bomb designed to disable any electronics in a small area.

"What is that?" Aspen asks.

"It's an electro-static shock bomb," Vex responds as Jared begins to open the box.

"A bomb!" Aspen yell whispers in fear of her life.

"Not a typical bomb; it won't hurt us. It disables all the power in the area of the blast. Probably will kill the power to the building. At least that's what we hope," Vex says.

"Won't the AFO come and investigate that?"

"They will, lets hope that they don't send the FP; and instead send the power guys," Jared says as he pulls the bomb out of the box. "Time is not our friend after this goes off Aspen."

Jared, Aspen, and Vex walk back over to the elevator where Placid is untangling the ropes on the grappling hooks they brought with them.

"Are you ready Placid?" Vex asks.

Placid nods his head that he is ready to go. Jared walks away from them and sets the bomb for a thirty second timer. Time ticks as Jared, Vex, Placid, and Aspen wait patiently with grappling hooks in their hands. They all put earplugs in to dampen the noise from the bomb.

Three…

Two…

One…

The electro bomb explodes sending electrical waves across the building. It is incredibly loud as the power shuts off across the building goes dark.

"Let's move," Jared says as he whips the grappling hook up and over the railing.

Everyone gets their hooks over except Aspen, who struggles throwing it up. Placid grabs her and has Aspen climb the one Jared threw, as he was almost to the top floor. Aspen starts her climb up the rope. She isn't even halfway up when the others are all up there. When Aspen reaches the top floor, Placid offers her a lending hand. After Placid lifts Aspen onto her two feet, she helps Placid pull up the grapple hooks and rope so they can be used to escape.

"Jared, the FP is on the way. You gotta hurry," Evan says on the radio to Jared.

"Shit!" Jared yells out loud. "We got a fed on the way, we gotta move faster, let's go."

Jared and Vex run up the stairs to the eighteenth floor to start going through the blueprints. Placid and Aspen walk to the back windows with the rope and grappling hooks. When they get there, Placid pulls an explosive device out of his backpack and secures it to the window. He motions for Aspen to wrap the grappling hooks around the columns to prepare for the descent down the outside. As Aspen is grabbing the rope, she sees a copy of The Island of Zufel in a glass case. The other author of the book, besides Ana W., is Tarrick W., a name that everyone in the world knows. Aspen shakes it out of her head as she wraps the hooks around the pillars.

Mel, still downstairs, hears the doors open by the FP and quickly disconnects her laptop which disconnects her camera control. She packs up her things, takes off her heels, and bolts to the elevator. As she runs across the main floor, she can hear the FP telling her to hit the floor or they'll shoot. Mel does not stop and starts to feel the bullets whizzing by her as she slides behind the elevator. She grabs her guns and her normal shoes out of her bag before she starts firing back.

Back upstairs in the library, Jared and Vex continue running through blueprints to find the ones for the Mimir as gunshots continue to ring out downstairs.

"More FP on the way. You gotta hurry," Evan says frantically on the radio. "The FP is sending a gunship."

"We're almost through the blueprints," Jared responds.

"Got it!" yells Vex as she lifts up the circular tube.

"Mel; get the fuck out of there! We're gonna blow the window," Jared radios.

"Working on it," Mel radios back.

Placid arms the bomb on the window as they all take cover behind the columns. The bomb detonates sending glass flying out the window. A shockwave causes books to fly off the shelves and the bookcases near the window get blown apart.

Everyone walks over broken glass with their rope as they walk up to the edge of the shattered window. Everyone puts on their gloves as they throw their ropes down the edge of the building. Aspen looks over the edge and steps backwards in fear, but Placid catches her and nudges her down the rope. Jared and Vex go first, sliding down the ropes through their gloves. Aspen goes next, and as she starts to slide down, she hears the sound of a gunship coming towards them. She slides down as fast as she can and looks up at Placid, who pulls out his assault rifle, aiming it at the gunship.

Mel continues to fire at the officers below as she hears the explosion upstairs. She uses the distraction to make a run for the doors. When she gets there, the doors are electronically locked, keeping her opening them. The FP move up and start shooting at her again, forcing her to take cover behind a bookcase.

Aspen makes it halfway down the building when she starts to hear Placid unleash his rifle on the gunship. She starts to book it as fast as she can down the rope. Aspen looks down and sees Jared and Vex yelling at her from the ground to hurry up.

Vex continues to yell at Aspen while Jared tries to rip open the doors to get Mel out, but the door won't budge. Mel comes over to try and pull the door open with Jared for more force, but while they are pulling, Mel takes a bullet through the head, splattering the window. Her lifeless body slides down the glass.

"Fuck!" Jared yells out.

Placid continues firing at the helicopter keeping it at bay until someone in the helicopter takes a single shot, hitting Placid in the chest, causing him to fumble forward and fall out of the window. Aspen is only ten feet from the bottom when Placid hits the ground splattering. Aspen screams as Jared and Vex get her off the rope. Aspen sees Mel, dead inside the library, causing her to nearly fall down as Jared drags her toward the car.

"No sympathy!" Jared yells in Aspen's face. "Let's go!"

Aspen runs following Jared as she looks back at Mel's body and into her lifeless eyes. Aspen has never seen a dead body before.

Jared, Vex, and Aspen run across the parking garage with the gunship in pursuit. Evan starts up the vehicle when he sees them running towards him; chomping at the bit to get going. Vex hops in the back with Jared. Aspen gets in the front seat next to Evan. The doors aren't even closed when Evan takes off down the road, keeping his headlights off.

÷

Charlie arrives to the NSA facility half dressed, as he goes into the control room, woken up by the overnight analysts.

"What's going on! Give me an update!" Charlie yells

"Team Bravo is in the gunship pursuing the suspects in a vehicle. The FP has killed two. Identifications are pending."

"Do we have a team in cars to track them?" Charlie asks.

"Yes sir. Two teams. Team Echo and Team Iota are enroute. Should be there momentarily."

÷

Evan drives quickly down the street so he can get onto the interstate and out of the city quickly before they get trapped. Smoke reels off the tires as he slides around corners. The gunship is tracking them with a search light while a shooter in the helicopter continually takes shots, hitting the SUV and the road. Jared and Vex crouch down in the backseat as a bullet smashes through the rear window, lodging itself in the fabric of the seat. Evan makes it to the ramp and drives onto the interstate with the gunship in tow. He drives quickly towards the forest where he can lose the gunship, swerving and swerving away from the gun shots. Vex messages Oscar and tells him to stay put until he hears from them.

As they cross the bridge to get out of downtown, two black SUVs pull up behind them from an onramp. The SUVs gain speed and rapidly close the gap between them.

"We have more company," Evan yells.

Jared and Vex look out the cracked back window as the SUVs close in on them. Vex pulls out her gun and Jared pulls out his revolver.

"Go faster!" yells Vex as she starts firing.

"I'm going as fast as I can!"

Vex and Jared unload at the SUVs behind them. The vehicles are bulletproof, however, so they start to take aim at the tires as they speed down the interstate. One SUV attempts to overtake their vehicle, but Jared gets a good shot at the tire, causing it slide to one direction and crash into the barriers on the side of the road. They are nearly to the forest and close to freedom.

The helicopter moves lower and attempts to fly even with the SUV before taking a final shot. The helicopter, still slightly above the SUV, fires a shot that hits Evan in the throat and grazes Aspen across her upper leg. The helicopter backs off and turns back toward the city instead of running into the trees. Evan starts gurgling out blood as he lifts one hand to his throat. Aspen screams as she grabs her leg with both hands. The vehicle slows down as it enters the forest, which allows the AFO to ram the back of their vehicle.

"Aspen! Get your foot on the gas! We need to get out of here!" Jared yells.

Aspen looks at Evan, who has blood squirting from his neck. He unbuckles his seatbelt, looks at Aspen and then pulls the door handle before throwing himself out onto the road. Aspen screams as the car shakes and she climbs into the blood-soaked driver's seat. Aspen puts her foot on the gas and grabs the door, all the while screaming and driving quickly down the road. Her leg feels like it is on fire as she alternates between looking at the road and her leg.

The AFO's vehicle drives right over Evan's body as they continue shooting and ramming the SUV. They pull up right next to Aspen forcing Aspen to ram into the vehicle with anger and hate as they go back and forth ramming each other. Eventually Aspen gets the upper hand and slams the vehicle into a guard rail around a corner, causing it to spin and roll out of control before smashing into a tree. Aspen keeps driving at neck-breaking speeds as she begins to cry.

Jared reaches his hand over the seat and puts his hand on Aspen's shoulder.

"We're gonna be ok Aspen. Pull over. We need to get off the road ASAP."

Aspen pulls off to the side of the road. Jared, Vex, and Aspen get out of the vehicle. Jared takes Aspen on his shoulder and starts to walk into the forest while Vex takes the SUV and drives it into the forest to hide it.

÷

"Get a dozen fucking teams in that goddamn forest. Right fucking now!" Charlie yells at the analysts. "Tear down that forest!"

Charlie rubs his hand over his face wiping the sweat away. Still half dressed, he walks to his office and sits down. Charlie debates calling the director right now or to wait a few hours with an update. He lays his arms down like a pillow on his desk and rests his head, trying to calm down his heart beat. Charlie decides to call Director Harlow. He would rather wake him up than not tell him until morning. He picks up his phone and calls Harlow to give him the news, hoping he is not killed for his failure.

"Yes Charlie," Harlow says as he answers the phone with a yawn

"We have a problem."

A few hours go by and Charlie paces outside Director Harlow's office to give him updates on the situation from the previous night. Charlie has changed into a suit he keeps in his office for this specific type of reason. He taps his feet and cracks his knuckles knowing that Harlow will walk around the corner at any moment.

Then he hears the footsteps. The solid, confident walk of the Director walking up the steps toward his office. Charlie sees Thomas Harlow, who is followed by his most trusted enforcer, Agent Leadheim. He walks into his office, followed by Charlie.

Director Harlow hangs his coat up by his desk before walking over to his liquor bar. Charlie walks in and sits down in front of the desk. Leadheim closes the door, locks it behind him, and puts his back to the door. Harlow pours a small drink and walks over to the window in his office. He opens the shades, puts one hand on his waist, and takes a sip.

"Tell me about the library," Director Harlow says.

"The ANA broke in and—"

"I know who it was. Tell me why they were there."

"They stole the blueprints for the Mimir."

"Hmm... interesting," Harlow says as he swirls his drink. "How did they get in?"

"They used a librarian's name tag. Her name is Susie Schaffer. Here's her file," Charlie says as he slides the file across the desk.

"Agent Leadheim. Please pay Ms. Schaffer a visit. Do you what you must," Harlow says as he passes the file to Leadheim.

"Yes sir," replies Leadheim as he takes the file and walks out the door.

“Lock the door Charlie,” Harlow says as he sits down in his chair. “I understand there were some casualties.”

“Yes sir. In the building we found a Ms. Melanie Taketa; shot. Outside the building, splattered on the concrete, was Mr. Arthur Drummer. Went by the name Placid. During a car chase, a man fell out of their vehicle. His name was Mr. Evan Recuri. He was shot through the neck,” Charlie says as he slides the files over the desk.

“Kill the families. Set the example.”

“Right away Sir,” Evan says with minor regret.

“Anyone else identified?”

“Yes, the cameras in the library were overridden, but we were able to get a peek at the three-surviving people in the vehicle from other cameras in the area,” Charlie says as he pulls two files from his bag.

“First, we have a Ms. Valerie Exero,” Charlie says as he slides the file across the desk. “Next is umm… Aspen James.”

“Humph. Of course. And the third person.”

“The third person was not able to be identified,” Charlie says as he grabs a picture from his tablet to show it to Harlow. “No records. Nothing.”

Harlow looks at the picture and puts a grim smile across his face and chuckles.

“Do you know who it is?” Charlie asks.

"I do. His name is Jared—"

Suddenly the phone starts to ring, cutting off Director Harlow. He looks over and sees the name on the caller info.

"Leave me Charlie," Harlow says.

Charlie closes the door as Director Harlow answers the phone, "Hello Tarrick.

Chapter 7

The trees start to look the same to Aspen as the sun starts to rise. Jared takes her off his shoulder and leans her in front of a large tree. Aspen grabs at her leg and cries out in pain. Jared leans over her leg while on his knees and looks the wound over. Vex slings her gun over her shoulder and gets down toward Aspen's wound next to Jared. As Vex starts to tear Aspen's pants around the wound and putting pressure on Aspen's leg, she starts to cry loud in agony. Jared puts his hand over Aspen's mouth and shushes her quiet.

Vex, with the wound now exposed, starts to clean it off with some water. She tears off a portion of her shirt to use as a bandage and pulls Aspen's leg up so she can better wrap it. Aspen cries out in pain through Jared's hand as Vex moves her leg. Jared grabs Aspen's hand and holds it with a vise-like grip as Vex wraps the cloth around the wound; pulling it tight and knotting it. Jared slowly moves his hand away from Aspen's mouth as Aspen quiets down with tears still dripping down her dirty face.

"Guess your more of a doctor than Oscar thinks," Aspen says as she wipes her face.

"Guess so," Vex responds.

"We gotta go," Jared says as he grabs Aspen up to her feet.

They continue deeper into the forest with no real sense of where they are going or where they will end up. Jared assumes they are far from their base of operations and most likely will not be able to return. He pushes them onward until he finds some sort of recognizable landmark.

÷

Agent Leadheim drives slowly through a quiet and old suburban town on the edge of the city called Ashburg. He looks over at the folder he has open on the passenger seat to confirm the address he is hunting for. As the house numbers decrease, Leadheim sees the house that he is looking for. He passes the faded yellow home and pulls up a few houses down and sits there looking in the rear-view mirror. Leadheim reaches into the backseat and grabs a briefcase and then sets it on his lap. Inside is a silenced pistol, which he pulls out and places on the center console of the car. There is also a black bag and some papers inside. Leadheim reaches over to the passenger seat where he closes the folder before slipping it into the briefcase. He shuts the briefcase and places it on the passenger seat before grabbing the pistol and placing it inside his coat jacket.

It is silent on the street with hardly any traffic or people on the pavement. Agent Leadheim steps out of the vehicle and walks up the sidewalk until he reaches the yellow house. The driveway is cracked and the landscaping is faded mulch with a few cherub and angel statues strewn about. Leadheim walks up the driveway and onto the path to the front door. He passes a picture window with its shades shut, walks up a couple steps and faces the front door. He adjusts his tie and reaches for the doorbell, which he rings. Leadheim steps back and folds his hands in front of him, waiting for the door to be answered.

Out if the corner of his eye, Leadheim sees the curtain move in the picture window. He reverts his attention to the door and hears the deadbolt unlock before the door opens to the chain length.

"What can I do for you?" a woman asks behind the door.

"I'm looking for Susie Schaffer."

"Why are you looking for Susie?"

"You know why. Now open the door and I won't kill everyone you love."

Susie pushes the door forward and removes the chain. Leadheim then pushes the door causing Susie to studder backwards into the living room, catching herself on the couch. He closes the door and pulls out his pistol.

"You are coming with me."

"You're an AFO bastard. I'm not coming with you. Just kill me you cocksucker. That's why you came here isn't it?"

"Don't. Make. This difficult," Leadheim says as he starts walking forward.

"Fuck you coward." Susie says before she spits toward Leadheim.

Leadheim, visually upset and disgusted, steps forward and pistol whips Susie on the side of her head, knocking her out. She falls off the couch and onto the floor. Leadheim looks around at the pictures of the Schaffer family throughout the room before he starts destroying them. He destroys the pictures and the frames around the living room in a bout of rage. As fast as his raging tantrum began; it stops. Leadheim adjusts his suit before stepping out through the front door and walking back to his vehicle.

Agent Leadheim starts up his vehicle and drives in reverse down the street and into Susie's driveway and up near the garage. He reaches over and opens his suitcase. He pulls out a black bag before stepping out and walking back into the house. Susie is still laid out on the floor as Leadheim steps over her and walks toward the garage. The garage is a two-car garage with Susie's car on one side and junk on the other. Leadheim walks through the garage until he finds a roll of duct tape. Before he walks back inside, Leadheim hits the button to open the garage door and opens the hatch on his vehicle.

He goes back inside and kneels down over Susie and sets the black bag off to the side. Leadheim starts by placing a piece of tape over her mouth. He rolls her over on her side and binds her arms behind her back and then binds her legs near her hips and around her ankles. Once she is bound, Leadheim takes the black bag and slides it over her head and tightening it loosely around her neck.

Leadheim picks Susie up, places her over his shoulder, and carries her towards the garage where he places her in the back of the vehicle. He closes the hatch, closes the garage door, and locks the front door before getting back in his vehicle. When he gets in his vehicle, he pauses for a moment before starting the vehicle up and driving off down the quiet road. As he drives, he decides to make a call to Charlie.

"What can I do for you Leadheim?" Charlie asks.

"I need you to find someone for me."

"Who?"

"Susie Schaffer's daughter. And her grandchildren. Have them brought to the Roq."

"Umm... ok."

Agent Leadheim hangs up the phone and Charlie feels sick to his stomach. Children... the Roq. Charlie knows what happens at the Roq, but only through rumors and hearsay. He has never been inside the black site and never wants to.

Leadheim drives across the inner city and towards the old dock district on the river. Full of warehouses and shipping containers the area was mostly abandoned until the AFO revived it. They rebuilt warehouses for storage according to the media, but the AFO built something else; a black site. These sites are only rumors to the public, but they are very real. The black sites are places of torture, death, and destruction. These sites are run by the Free States American Military, or F-SAM. This site is called the Roq.

Agent Leadheim pulls up to a guarded gate where two guards, dressed in black military style gear and armed with rifles, watch the gate. He rolls down his window so the guards can see his face. They open the gate and let him drive in. Leadheim visits the Roq often enough to not show his ID badge to the guards. As he drives in, the guards shut the gate behind him. Leadheim drives across a vast sea of concrete until he drives up to a large warehouse covered in lights along the river. He pulls up to a large garage door that opens up immediately allowing him to drive in. Once inside the warehouse, he drives around mountains of shipping containers, stacked to the ceiling. He pulls up in front of a group of four with the initials ROQ on them, indicating the brand of shipping container. Suddenly the doors are opened by a group of soldiers allowing Leadheim to drive into the containers.

Once the doors are shut, the elevator activates and brings Agent Leadheim and the soldiers down several floors until they reach a large room. Leadheim drives the SUV into the room and gets out of the vehicle to speak with the soldiers.

"There is a woman in the back. Bring her to room seven. Strip her and attach her to a chair," Leadheim says as the soldiers pull Susie out of the SUV, who is now awake and kicking. "When her party arrives, put them in room six. Gag and bag them. No one touches or harms them. Understand!"

"Yes sir."

Leadheim walks over to Susie, loosens the bag, and pulls it off her head.

"Welcome to the Roq."

Two soldiers carry Susie who is kicking her legs as hard as she can and trying to scream through the duct tape. Her eyes dart around everywhere as they go through a swing door and down a long hallway. Susie watches as Leadheim disappears as the swing doors shut. She continues to struggle as she watches the numbers on the wall steadily increase until they reach room seven. One soldier opens the door for the two carrying Susie. Once she is in the room, the soldier holding the door open shuts it and walks inside to help the others.

Agent Leadheim's phone rings. He looks at it and sees that it is Charlie.

"Yes Charlie."

"Susie's daughter and grandchildren are enroute to the Roq. Her son-in-law was also there. The team took him as well. Should be there in the next ten minutes."

"Good."

Leadheim hangs up the phone and walks to his vehicle and opens the door to the backseat after grabbing his briefcase. With the briefcase open and laying on the seat, Leadheim folds his coat and lays it into his briefcase. He pulls out a leather bag and sets it off to the side on the floor of the vehicle. Leadheim's tie fits snuggly into the briefcase next to the suit and the black hood. He shuts the door and paces the floor until the family arrives. The elevator arrives and a van comes into the room and parks towards the hallway. Leadheim can hear the muffled screams as it goes by him.

Agent Leadheim asks the team driving the van which one the husband is and tells the soldiers to keep him there. Other soldiers carry the daughter and grandchildren through the swing doors and down to room six. Two soldiers drag the man in front of Leadheim, who takes the hood off to see a scared man on his knees with duct tape over his mouth.

"Your useless to me," Leadheim says as he shoots the man in the head.

The man's body slumps onto the floor. Blood starts to pool around his head on the white marble floor. His eyes remain open, staring toward the hallway. Leadheim tells the soldiers to incinerate the man's body as he walks toward his vehicle. He grabs the leather bag he took from his briefcase and starts walking toward the hallway as two soldiers grab the dead man by the arms and legs and carry him to a door off to the side.

Leadheim pushes the swing doors open and walks down the well-lit white marble hallway towards room six, where a soldier stands guard outside. He reminds him that they do not touch anyone in the room. The guard confirms he understands as Leadheim walks to room seven, where Susie is being held. The guard opens the door for Leadheim and shuts it behind him.

The room is bright white, just like the hallway. A 1000 square foot room with a small pile of clothes in the corner and a stripped down, naked woman zip tied to a metal chair in the middle. Susie has a boulder of a bump on her head where Leadheim hit her. She stares at him with deep contempt and immense hatred as he walks slowly across the soundproof room and kneels down in front of her.

"Those men said they were going to rape me. Then decided my wrinkled body was not worth their time," Susie says as a tear rolls down her face.

"Do you say that because you think I care."

"You don't care. You're a pathetic excuse for a person."

"Hmm," Leadheim says as he slaps Susie across the face. "Tell me where to find the ANA?"

"I don't know. Even if I did, I wouldn't tell the likes of you."

"I figured this was how this was going to play out with you."

Leadheim reaches over and grabs the leather bag he had brought in. He undoes the leather strap and rolls it out in front of him. Inside is a plethora of sharp blades and construction tools. Susie's heart rate starts going up and her breathing gets more erratic as Leadheim pulls out a tin snip and stands up in front of her.

"Where is the ANA?" Leadheim asks as he taps the tin snip in the palm of his hand.

Susie spits toward Leadheim and does not respond. Leadheim slides his tongue in his cheek as he looks Susie directly in the eyes. He kneels down grabs her left hand and puts her pinky in the snip, cutting it off slowly. Susie screams in agony as her pinky falls to the ground covered in blood. Leadheim continues to ask about the ANA; and Susie continues to resist. After a few fingers, Leadheim becomes bored and abandons the tin snips. He grabs a well-sharpened knife.

"Let's try something else," Leadheim says as he flips the knife in his hands in front of Susie.

÷

The sun is reaching its high point across the forest and shimmers light through the trees. Aspen, Jared, and Vex continue walking through the vast national forest to outrun the AFO. As they climb over fallen trees and nearly break their ankles on rocks, they hear the faint sound of running water. Vex rushes ahead to scout while Jared and Aspen slowly walk together on Jared's weight. As they get closer, they can hear the sound of water getting louder. Eventually Jared and Aspen reach a drop off that leads down to a river below. Vex is already nearly there gasping for a drink. She whips her gun over her back, goes to her knees, and starts gulping the cold mountain water.

Jared and Aspen slowly start making their way down a less steep area where Vex went down. As they make their way down, Vex suddenly snaps up and runs back to Aspen and Jared.

"I see a bridge to the South. It's far, but if the AFO have anyone watching from there with scopes; they could see us," Vex says.

Aspen and Jared finish making it down the slope with the help of Vex. Jared takes out a pair of binoculars and gets down low as he crawls toward the rocky edge of the river bank. He crawls until he can get a good view of the bridge.

"I think I see soldiers checking cars. Looks like they have a checkpoint set up. I don't see anybody else though," Jared says. "How bout you sneak out there and fill up your bottle for everyone to share Vex."

Jared stands up and runs back into cover as Vex runs out to the river to fill her water bottle. Jared lays Aspen up against a tree as Vex runs back to give Aspen the bottle of water. Vex then moves in to redo the wrap over her bullet wound. She tears her shirt again and then removes the piece of cloth she had put on earlier that day.

"The bleeding has mostly stopped, but Aspen still needs Oscar to make sure the wound doesn't get infected," Vex says as she ties the new cloth around Aspen's leg.

While not nearly as painful as before, Aspen still grunts quietly as Vex ties the cloth tight.

"Thank you," Aspen says to Vex as Vex moves backwards and sits atop a rock near Jared.

"So... what now guys. We can't cross the river in the shape we're in," Vex says. "Current is too strong."

"We don't need to cross. I recognize where we are," Jared says. "This is the Canawa River. And that bridge is the Grandel Bridge."

"And...?" Aspen asks.

"I'm getting to that," Jared says. "I know of a cave we can go to. Somewhere my mom used to bring me. It's South of here though. Past the bridge."

"Why don't we backtrack a bit and cross at the road instead of the bridge?" Aspen asks. "When its dark, they shouldn't see us."

"There's a canyon over there," Jared says. "We need to wait four or five hours until it's real dark. Then we'll cross. Let's start moving that direction."

÷

Susie rages awake with a huge breath of air after Leadheim stabs her in the heart with adrenaline. She is wide awake and in screaming in pain. Leadheim is taking his time with her and made sure she would stay alive. All of her fingers are gone except for her thumbs. Her toes are all cut off. The taste of bile fills her mouth as she throws up on her already stained chest. Blood drips from her head and from all over her body.

"Have you had enough Susie?" Leadheim asks as he gets up close to her face.

"I... I don't. I don't know anything," mutters Susie.

"Tell me where the ANA is!" Leadheim screams in her face.

"I don't. I... I don't."

Leadheim stands up and starts walking towards the door.

"Bring me her family!" Leadheim yells down the hall after opening the door.

Leadheim walks back over to Susie and stands next to her as the soldiers drag her family into the room. They are gagged and bagged just like Leadheim had requested with duct tape around their ankles and wrists behind their backs. There are two children and an adult woman, Susie's daughter. Two soldiers are holding the daughter and two are holding the kids; one per kid.

Agent Leadheim walks over to the taller child and pulls him away from the soldier and brings him in front of Susie. Leadheim takes off the hood so Susie can see him. He wasn't any older than twelve, not even a teenager. His screams are muffled by the duct tape over his mouth.

"Look at your grandma. This is her fault," Leadheim says to the boy as he grabs him up by the hair.

Leadheim takes the knife in his hand and stabs the young boy in the throat. His eyes are full of fear as Leadheim drops him to the ground with blood gushing from his throat and leaking from the duct tape around his mouth. He wriggles around on the ground until he stops moving.

Susie cries out in pain for her grandson with blood-soaked tears coming from her eyes.

"Tell me what I want to know Susie," Leadheim says as he grabs the other child from the soldier.

"I... I don't know... anything. I swear. Please... please stop," Susie cries out.

Leadheim drags the child by the hair and brings him right in front of Susie before removing the hood. It is another boy, no older than six or seven. Leadheim rips off the duct tape from the boy's mouth and immediately starts crying to his grandma.

"They... they only contacted me... when they needed... needed me. I... I don't know... I don't know where they... they hide. Please... stop. Please stop."

"Who contacted you, Susie?" Leadheim asks as he dangles the knife in front of the screaming boy.

"I... I don't know... I don't know his name."

"Not good enough."

Leadheim stabs the little boy in throat just like the last boy and drops him to die on Susie's lap. He bleeds out all over her gurgling blood. Susie cries in exhaustion and starts to pass out before Leadheim jabs her with more adrenaline to keep her awake. She blasts up, almost out of the chair and Leadheim walks up and crouches behind her.

"What's his name?" Leadheim whispers in Susie's ear. "Where did you meet him?"

"I'm... done talking to you. There is nothing... nothing you can... do to me."

"I doubt that," Leadheim says as his eyes get really big.

He stands up and nods to the soldiers holding onto Susie's daughter. The soldiers remove the bag over her head and start hitting her as they remove her clothes. The soldiers strip all of her clothes and begin abusing the daughter. Susie shuts her eyes, but Leadheim grabs her head and holds open her eyes, forcing her to watch her daughter get violated by the four soldiers. Tears come from her eyes, not from being held open, but from the purest sadness imaginable.

“You will never win,” Leadheim whispers to Susie before he releases her eyes and stabs her in the throat from behind.

Susie’s head drops down as the limited amount of blood she still had drains from her neck.

“Once you’re done with her; kill her and burn all the bodies,” Leadheim tells the soldiers as he leaves the room.

÷

It is very dark outside in the forest. The only light comes from the moon peeking over the trees and reflecting on the river. Vex, Jared, and Aspen creep along the edge of the river in the forest toward the Grandel Bridge. Vex takes the lead while Jared watches over Aspen, who is attempting to mostly walk by herself, but remains slow moving. The AFO has spot lights set up on the bridge to warn cars to stop and secede to a search. With no idea how many soldiers they may encounter, the group needs to be ready for anything.

They approach the bridge and go slower than they were. Vex does her best to point out hazards to the other two, but since it is dark, it makes it difficult. Once they get nearby where they can hear voices, Jared whispers to Aspen to hang back while him and Vex take care of the situation. Aspen hangs back and finds a place to sit down.

Vex and Jared continue up the embankment. As they get closer, they start to make out the voices and determine there is at least three different people speaking. Once they reach flatter ground, Jared and Vex get down to a crawl and get behind some brush to assess the bridge. As they expected, they see a single soldier, a female, and two male soldiers. They are all wearing the usual forest camouflage with the AFO insignias emblazoned on their arms; it is the F-SAM. All three are carrying assault rifles, but do not have them at the ready. Vex and Jared decide to watch them for a while to see if any other soldiers are around or on patrol.

"Maybe we can slip by unnoticed," Vex whispers. "They appear pretty distracted."

"I'm not willing to take the chance. We need to kill them."

"They're kids Jared."

"What is three lives to a national reckoning," Jared whispers. "We kill them; take the weapons. That's it."

"I suppose you're right. What's the play then?"

"You crawl up closer over there near the bridge. I'll go left; down a way and get their attention. Once they start coming my direction, step out and open fire."

"What if they don't all go? I wouldn't."

"Then figure it out," Jared whispers as he turns to the left and starts crawling.

Vex starts making her way closer to the bridge and closer to the soldiers. She goes slowly and tries to make the least amount of sound possible. About halfway to where she wants to be, Vex hears Jared making sounds down the road grabbing the soldier's attention.

The soldiers all look down the road toward Jared. One pulls out a flashlight while the other two get their rifles ready to fire. He shines the flashlight down the road and scans the area. They don't see anything and discuss the sound amongst each other. Jared then makes more noise, which prompts the female soldier to send the male soldiers to investigate. They point their guns toward Jared and flip their lights on that are attached to their guns. Vex is now in a better position. The female officer starts slowly walking towards Jared behind the others. As soon as the time is right, Vex jumps out and shoots the female soldier, dropping her to the pavement. The other soldiers turn around, but Vex is already firing upon them. Jared runs out of the bushes once their down and finds one soldier barely breathing. Jared puts a single shot into his head to make sure he stays down.

"Good job Vex. You collect the guns. I'll help Aspen up," Jared says as he runs into the forest yelling for Aspen.

"Got it."

Vex runs over to the soldiers grabbing their rifles and side arms. She also grabs one of their radios so she can listen in on the radio channels and hopefully keep the group one step ahead. Jared runs into the forest and runs into Aspen, who is already making her way up the embankment. Jared tries to get Aspen to lean on his shoulder and help walk her up to the bridge, but she throws his arm off, insisting she can do it herself. Once they get to the road, Vex hands them weapons to carry and they quickly traverse the embankment on the other side.

They quickly make it down to the river and begin traveling South towards the cave Jared knows about. As they walk, they don't hear anything on the radio, which is a good sign. Unfortunately, a patrol or a civilian could come across it and call it in anytime, forcing them to keep moving at a decent pace.

Vex hops the rocks quickly, staying ahead of the group with two guns thrown over her shoulder and a pistol jammed into her pants. Jared stays behind her and closer to Aspen, who is now carrying an assault rifle over her shoulder. They keep going until Jared has them stop because he thinks they are close to the cave.

Jared looks back toward the bridge, which is half a mile away now. He walks around the riverbank looking for a specific rock that he used as a kid to help identify the location of the cave. He had never been outside the cave when it was dark so it was a much more difficult task. Eventually Jared spots the rock sticking out closer to the water then he remembers. The rock is a taller rock sticking up that is split down the center, forming the shape of a V. Jared walks up to it and looks toward the river and then toward the shore. He stands parallel to the stone and starts walking toward the embankment leading into the forest. Aspen and Vex follow Jared as he leaves the rocks and goes into the forest. He stops at a tree with large roots.

The tree is massive and the roots are above the ground with smaller roots growing and hanging from it. Jared takes the rifle off his back and pushes past the roots into an open space. He flips the light on the rifle revealing the depth of the cave. Aspen and Vex follow Jared through the roots and follow him around a couple curves into a larger space in the cave system.

"Home sweet home," Jared says as he walks into the space.

Jared shines the light around the room trying to recollect his memory of the cave. He looks down and sees a few rocks loosely aligned in a circle with half burned logs in the center.

"Let's collect the rocks and rebuild this fire pit," Jared says as he walks to the edge of the room and finds a pile of firewood stacked up.

He grabs a couple logs and brings it over to Vex and Aspen who have the fire pit mostly fixed and ready to burn. Jared arranges the logs and pulls out his lighter and cigarettes. First, he lights up a smoke and inhales a long drag, holding the nicotine in before he breathes out. He takes a few smaller drags from the cigarette before setting the lighter down and ripping pieces off his shirt for kindling. Aspen and Vex also rip off pieces of clothing to add to the fire.

Once they have some clothing under the logs, Jared takes his lighter and lights up a piece of his shirt before tossing it in. The flames slowly start to spread across the various colors of wool and cotton until the logs catch fire. Soon, the fire is going smoothly and Jared grabs more logs to keep it going. He stares into the flames and memories start floating back to him.

Jared snaps out of his trance suddenly when he hears Aspen speaking about paintings on the wall. Aspen points out paintings of stick people and ships and trees. Then she sees the name Jared painted on the walls.

"Jared; how much time did you spend here?" Aspen asks.

"Quite a bit. My mom would keep me here when she was out."

"What was she doing when she went out?" Aspen asks as she sits down across from Jared at the fire.

"Resistance stuff. Scouting, attacking, I don't know. I never knew. I only remember her face when she would come and bring me home from this cave. She was always happy to see me."

"Jared's mom was the first person to resist the AFO openly after they won the elections in 2220. Absolute badass," Vex chimes in.

"What happened to her?"

"That's a long story," Jared says. "Let's get some sleep."

"Did Tarrick Welch do something to her?"

Jared's eyes grow large before he stands up and steps across the fire towards Aspen. The veins in Jared's face are deep red and Aspen can see the hatred in his eyes.

"Never mention his name in front of me," Jared says as he points down at Aspen.

"Ok. Ok," Aspen says quickly as she holds her hands up to surrender.

Jared storms off out of the room in the cave and out of sight.

"Don't say anything about that to him. Let's just go to sleep and get back at it tomorrow."

Aspen agrees with Vex and lies down trying to find a comfortable position, but cannot fall asleep. Her mind is filled with theories on Jared, his mother Ana, and the likes of Tarrick Welch. Another ten minutes goes by and Aspen still cannot fall asleep. Aspen looks around the cave. Vex is snoring and Jared has not come back. Aspen slowly stands up in hopes of not waking up Vex and creeps toward the entrance of the cave. As she rounds the corner, she runs into Jared who is sitting down on a rock jutting out of the cave wall.

"I'm sorry. For yelling and everything," Jared says.

There is an awkward silence between the two as Aspen sits down next to Jared.

"I need to know. It's... bothering me."

Jared looks at Aspen and thinks before he speaks.

"Tarrick is my father. At least that's what my mother told me."

"Holy shit."

"They wrote The Island of Zufel together while they were married. To my mom it was simply a book, but to Tarrick... it became an obsession. He quickly gained a following using the books outline for creating a supposed utopia. The Strausser Law in 2212 gave him a massive boost in popularity. With that, the AFO became the dominant party in the country. The election in 2020 is when Tarrick Welch became president and the rest you know."

"Woah. That's heavy."

"Yeah. So, uh... my mom opposed what he was doing and they argued and fought until she left him while she was pregnant with me. Six years later Tarrick was president and my mom hated him and fought back. Along with a lot of other people."

"Did he kill her? Your mom?" Aspen asks as she rubs Jared's back.

"Um... I can't. I can't talk about that right now," Jared says as he rubs his hands over his face. "Another time perhaps. Let's get some sleep."

Jared stands up and then assists Aspen in getting up as well. The two walk back to the room in the cave where Vex remains asleep with a slightly louder snore than before. They both lay down in the most comfortable positions they can get into and slowly fall asleep as the fire settles down into embers.

Chapter 8

Charlie wakes up in his apartment to the sun glimmering through his curtains. The vents blowing cool air kept blowing them apart and sending rays of light into his eyes. He rolls over multiple times trying to keep his eyes closed and puts his comforter over his head. His phone starts to ring and he starts to groan. Charlie reaches through his blanket to grab his cellphone and sees Director Harlow's name on the screen. He collects himself and rubs his eyes before answering.

"Good morning, Sir."

"Charlie. Some F-SAM soldiers were killed at a checkpoint in the forest last night. I need you here to coordinate the search for these traitors."

"I'll be there."

"Good."

Harlow hangs up the phone and Charlie sets his phone back on the nightstand. He stretches upward before sliding out from under his comforter and stepping slowly towards the bathroom. Charlie takes a quick shower, brushes his teeth, puts on deodorant, and get dressed for work. He grabs his phone, his keys, and his suitcase after he gets dressed. Charlie walks to the entryway in his high-rise apartment and into the hallway of the building before walking to the elevator.

As he goes down the elevator, Charlie pulls out his phone and notices he has messages from an anonymous phone number. Charlie doesn't open them, but instead slides them away, deleting them. Charlie places his phone in his pocket again after reaching the garage floor. He walks toward his car, gets in, and starts driving to the NSA. Once Charlie puts his car in autonomous mode, he takes out his phone again to check his emails. He has more texts from an anonymous number. Charlie deletes it and continues on.

Charlie arrives to the NSA complex and switches his car into manual mode. With the buildings in the distance overshadowing the trees, Charlie pulls up to the main gate. He drives into the large building the main gate is housed in and drives onto the moving walkway before getting out. It's a large concrete structure with guards out front and guards on top. Tall concrete barriers laden with barb wire stretch around the entire compound standing twenty feet tall. Every car going into the NSA, goes through a large scanner that x-rays the vehicle from each side and top to bottom.

While his car goes through the scanner, Charlie walks through a security checkpoint. He removes his coat and shoes before walking through a scanner. Charlie walks through the scanner and is then subjected to a pat down by a guard. After Charlie is cleared, he picks up his phone, keys, and other accessories he had in his pockets that got hand felt and searched. Once Charlie is past security, he walks over to his car that is now done being scanned and gets in to drive the quarter mile to the complex.

The road to the complex is two lanes and has trees lining the sides. Charlie drives it almost every day with the occasional day off. He pulls into the parking lot and goes to his assigned parking space. Tall office buildings surround the main courtyard where the Mimir is located, which has its own parking lot. Charlie walks off to his building and goes to the elevator that brings him down to his office.

When the elevator stops, Charlie steps off and walks into the command center.

"Where are we at with the search?" Charlie asks Greg.

"Multiple teams are searching the forest on foot, Sir," Greg says.

"Put the map up on the screen."

"Debra," Greg says as he points to an analyst. "Put it up."

"Ok, Sir. Everything highlighted in red has been searched and everything yellow is currently being searched."

"Where were the F-SAM soldiers were killed?"

"Right there," Greg says as he points a laser pointer at the map on Grandel Bridge.

"No evidence. Nothing."

"Nothing."

"Well... keep searching. Let me know."

Charlie walks out of the command center and into his office to give Director Harlow an update on the situation. He sits down to call when his cell phone starts to buzz. It's an anonymous number. He quickly ends the call and puts his phone on silent before he dials up Harlow.

÷

Nothing has happened to Nolan and Aspen as they sit in their house waiting. The AFO brings them groceries to eat, since they are not allowing the couple or their children to leave. They are glued to the news waiting on more information about the attack of the library by the ANA from the other day. Aspen seems to be much more concerned than Nolan is. Nolan keeps the kids playing in the basement out if fear of a bomb or missile attack.

Nolan, frustrated about not getting any information directly from the ANA decides to have a chat with Agent F in the garage.

"Hey... can we talk for just a second?" Nolan asks as he opens the door.

"What is it?"

"I need information. I'm going crazy here."

"I don't have any information."

"Bullshit!" Nolan yells out.

"Excuse me," Agent F says as he stands up in Nolan's face.

"Sorry," Nolan says as he backs up and raises his hands. "I just need something to help calm me down. Aspen is going nuts. I'm going nuts."

"I will have someone call you."

"Ok."

"Go back inside."

Nolan goes back into the house as quickly as possible. Agent F calls into the NSA command center.

÷

The sun starts to set and paints colors across the sky. The forest becomes quiet again from what Jared can tell as he listens and watches through the roots covering the cave. Jared wants to move in the dark and follow the river until they reach the outskirts of the Iron City. From there, their plan is to get a car and reconnect with Oscar, who they hoped was not dead. Jared is thinking that Oscar would have traveled to the nearest safe house the night they did not return from the library.

Without phone service this deep in the forest, they are unable to send or receive any messages. Once they get closer to the city, they should be able to communicate.

Once the sun has been gone for a few hours, Jared, Vex, and Aspen leave the safety of the cave and traverse the rocky terrain along the river. Aspen has much more mobility now, but is still slower than the others. Vex takes the lead with Jared behind her, who keeps a close eye on Aspen. Navigating the rocks in the dark is not an easy task as they stumble multiple times.

Several hours later, in the middle of the night, the light emanating from the city starts to lighten up the sky. If Jared's estimates are correct, they will arrive into the town of Needham, a suburb of Iron City, very shortly. Vex puts her phone on silent so it doesn't start ringing when she comes across done cell service.

As they get closer to Needham, Vex's phone receives text messages from Oscar wondering if they are ok and where they are. He mentions in one of his messages that he will be at the safe house in Ryder, which is nearby where they parked for the library operation.

The group starts approaching some houses in Needham. Vex goes ahead to scout while Jared and Aspen hang back. Vex looks around for any vehicles parked outside that would be inconspicuous. She finds a midsized car that is sitting in the street where it is not well lit. The town of Needham is an affluent neighborhood and is full of newer homes that fringe on the border of the forest.

Vex walks away from the car and back through the backyard of a house to grab Jared and Aspen. They creep through the yard together where Jared and Aspen wait by the gate while Vex attempts to break into the car. It is easier if she has the right tools, but nothing Vex has works to open the doors. Vex looks around at the houses looking for something she can use to wedge the door open, but is unable to find anything. She walks back over to Jared and Aspen to determine their next course of action.

"We need to break into a house," Jared whispers.

"What if we run into someone?" Aspen asks.

"Let's hope we don't. Come on," Vex says as she starts moving towards a house hunched down.

Vex takes the lead as they sneak up to the front door of the house with the car they want out front. Vex pulls a bobby pin out of her hair and kneels down to work the lock on the door. With the threat of a house alarm, Jared tells Aspen to hang back while him and Vex go inside. Vex signifies she is ready to turn the lock and Jared nods that he is ready as he walks right up to the door.

Vex turns the lock and pushes open the door slowly to see if there is alarm. After the door opens a few inches, an alarm starts beeping, not loud enough to notify neighbors, but enough to wake the homeowners. Jared rushes in with Vex right on his tail. Vex moves past the living room and heads down a set of stairs while Jared rushes the other side of the living room towards what he believes to be bedrooms. Jared finds people first and comes out of a room with an older male and female. He puts the gun to their heads demanding they turn the alarm off. Aspen slips into the house and locks the door behind her as Jared forces the man to shut off the alarm.

"Hey," Jared says to Aspen. "Put your gun on them."

Aspen lifts a pistol up at the man and woman in the living room, who are now on the floor. Vex comes up the stairs with two teenagers in front of her and has them sit on the floor with the older couple, who are their parents. They all embrace each other as the daughter begins to cry out loud. Vex turns the lights on in the living room as they all put their guns on the family.

"Put your fucking hands up! Is that your car on the street?" Jared asks the man.

"No... no. That's the neighbor's car," studders the man.

"Where are your keys?" Jared asks.

"In... in the kitchen."

"Hey you," Jared says to Aspen. "Go find their car keys in the kitchen."

Aspen goes into the kitchen to find the keys and sees them hanging on the wall near the door to the garage. She grabs both sets and brings them back to the living room.

“There are two vehicles,” Aspen says as she shows the keys to Jared and Vex.

“Go into the garage and find something to tie these people up with,” Jared says as he nods his head to Vex. “You keep an eye out front. Make sure no one’s watching.”

“Please don’t kill us,” the older woman pleads to Jared.

“Just don’t test me and you’ll be fine.”

Vex comes back from the garage with duct tape and some electrical cords to bind the family of four. Vex plans to use duct tape to bind them individually and then tie them together to the banister using the electrical cords. When she is done tying up the family, Vex goes toward the garage with Aspen. There is a bigger car and then a bigger SUV. Vex hops in the driver’s seat and starts up the vehicle while Aspen gets in the front seat next to her. She hooks up her phone to the vehicles operating system and begins hacking the SUV.

“What are you doing?” Aspen asks.

“I’m overriding the SUVs server so I alone can control it.”

“So, you’re hacking the car so the AFO can’t stop it remotely.”

“Yeah.”

“That’s crazy.”

"Crazy cool. And… it's done. Go open the garage door."

Aspen gets out of the car and hits the button to open the garage door. Vex unhooks her phone and slowly backs up the SUV into the driveway where Aspen gets in. They wait in the SUV until Jared comes out of the house a few minutes later. The garage door closes and Jared rolls out. Jared jogs to the SUV and lays down in the backseat so no one can see him. Vex backs up out of the driveway and into the road being careful not to rev the engine to hard.

They drive through the neighborhood at the speed limit to not attract any unnecessary attention to themselves. The houses they pass can be considered mansions or vacation homes. Most do not have lights on inside except for a couple. Vex drives until she reaches a highway and can find her grip on where they are exactly. Once she gets on the highway and is able to locate a few landmarks; Vex plots a course to the safe house in Ryder where Oscar is most likely hiding out.

The roads are without traffic as it starts to rain again. They pass a few cars here and there as Vex drives out of Needham and through the other affluent suburbs. Vex drives across the bridge into the city and rides the highway west toward Ryder. Once she passes the downtown skyscrapers and condos, Vex drives into the real downtown. She exits the highway and tells Aspen to keep her eyes sharp in case anyone approaches the car.

Vex pulls the SUV into an alley alongside a run-down apartment building with smashed windows and a crumbling foundation. They shut down the car and wait for a second as they watch the rain pour and the people walking the sidewalks. Vex gets out first with Aspen, followed by Jared. They walk towards the back of the alley where a back door leads into the building.

The hallway they walk into smells of rot and decay as rainwater drips through the building collecting on the floor in puddles. Water spots stain the walls they pass as Vex leads them toward the stairs with a rifle drawn. They walk up the creaky steps up to the third floor, where an exposed light bulb flickers in the hallway. At the end of the hallway is the room D5, which is the safe house. Vex walks up to the door and knocks three times randomly.

They hear movement from inside the apartment moving towards them; then the door unlocks. The door slowly opens and Oscar peeks around the edge of the door, verifying who it is before opening the door wide.

"I told you it was a good idea to create a special knock," Oscar says as he opens the door for them and starts giving them hugs. "It's so good to see you. All of you."

Everybody walks into the apartment before Oscar closes the door and locks it shut. The apartment is as run down as the building is with holes in the walls and ripped up flooring. There are a few pieces furniture in the apartment including a blaze orange couch, a brown recliner, and an old TV on a stand.

“Can you look at my leg Oscar?” Aspen asks as she lays down on the couch.

Oscar starts unwrapping Aspen’s leg of the cloth Vex wrapped around it. Once he finishes unwrapping it, Oscar looks at the bullet graze wound for a moment.

“Guess you’re more of a doctor than I thought, Vex.” Oscar says.

“Appreciate it.”

“I need to you to grab me the vodka from the kitchen, Vex,” Oscar says. “I also need some bandages and the knife from the first aid box over there.”

“How bad is this going to hurt?” Aspen asks nervously.

“Pretty bad I would imagine,” Oscar says.

“Don’t you have like a sedative or something?”

“This is not a hospital Aspen. Ah; thank you Vex,” Oscar says as Vex hands him the supplies.

“Drink some of this vodka,” Jared says as he grabs the vodka from the floor and hands it to Aspen.

“That’s not what’s it’s for,” Oscar says as he grabs the vodka from Jared’s hand. “That will thin your blood and I need you to clot. You want to clot.”

Oscar takes the knife and sets it on Aspen’s stomach before he grabs the vodka off the floor. He takes the lid off and drops it on the floor.

"Ok. Jared, I need you to hold Aspen down and cover her mouth so she can scream. Vex, hold her legs as still as possible," Oscar says to them before talking to Aspen. "Aspen, this will take me maybe twenty; maybe thirty seconds. Don't flail around. I need you to not flail."

Aspen nods her head to Oscar as she starts taking deep breathes. Vex grabs her legs and puts all of her weight into them. Jared brings his arm across her chest and the brings his hand on his other arm over her mouth in anticipation of screams. Aspen clutches Jared's arm that is draped across her. She notices his hands are full of blood, but before she can say anything, Oscar starts pouring vodka over her leg.

Jared puts his hand over Aspen's mouth as she screams into it and pulls hard on his arm in agony. Oscar takes the knife off her and starts cutting all the dead skin away around Aspen's leg, adding more vodka after every few cuts. He moves as quick as he can soaking up fresh blood and cleaning the wound. Once Oscar is almost done and getting ready to wrap up the wound, Aspen passes out from exhaustion. Jared checks her vital signs and verifies she is ok before they lift up her leg for Oscar to wrap.

Oscar grabs a few pillows and places them under her leg so it can stay elevated. He checks Aspens breathing and heart rate; confirming that she is ok. Vex and Jared assist Oscar by wiping up the excess blood on the floor and the couch.

“I’m gonna wash my hands,” Jared says as he walks to the bathroom.

“Let’s get some sleep. We’ll figure everything out in the morning. Got it?”

Oscar agrees and leads Vex to the bedroom. The bedroom has multiple sleeping bags on top of mats on the floor with a single lumpy pillow per bag. Vex immediately lays down and attempts to get comfortable and pass out while Oscar goes to the bathroom to clean up with Jared.

“You almost done?” Oscar asks as he peeks into the bathroom. “I need to wash my hands too.”

“Go wash them in the kitchen.”

“I can’t. The pipes are broken. The bathroom has the only water.”

“It’ll be a minute,” Jared says as he scrubs his hands harder with the bottom of his shirt.

“Vex and I agreed to go to sleep and talk about everything tomorrow.”

“Ok. I’ll stay up and wait for Aspen to wake up,” Jared says as he dries his hands and steps past Oscar.

“Don’t get attached.”

“I’m not attached,” Jared says as he sits down in the recliner next to Aspen.

Chapter 9

The next morning, Aspen opens her eyes to light coming through a crack in the newspapers tacked to the windows. She tries to move her leg, which is sore as hell, causing her to scream softly, but loud enough to wake up Jared, who is in the recliner nearby.

"You, ok?" Jared asks as he sits up in the recliner.

Aspen nods her head and looks up at the spotted ceiling above her head as she tries to adjust her eyes to the light. She doesn't hear any movement in the apartment and assumes everyone is still asleep.

"Do you know what time it is?" Aspen asks Jared with her eyes closed.

"It's around seven," Jared responds as he lights up a cigarette.

"Are you really going to smoke in here?"

Jared looks around at the stained walls and wrecked flooring before looking back at Aspen and smoking his cigarette.

"Have you seen this place?"

"I suppose you're right," Aspen says as she hears a door slowly open out of her view.

Oscar walks out yawning and goes directly to the bathroom. He uses the toilet without shutting the door and Aspen can hear it happen. Before he starts undressing for a shower, however, Oscar does shut the door. Aspen hears the shower start to sputter before it gives way to the water from the shower head. As Oscar is taking a shower, Aspen hears Vex come out of the bedroom and open the door to the bathroom.

"Dammit Vex! You could have knocked," Oscar yells out.

"Holy shit Oscar. I've seen it before," Vex says as she closes the door to the bathroom.

Vex comes out of the bathroom shorty after and walks over to the kitchen to get something to drink. With a bottle of water in her hand, Vex comes over and sits on the arm rest of the couch. She takes a few big gulps from the water bottle before passing it to Aspen, who then passes it to Jared. Vex stands up, walks over to the TV, and changes channels until she gets to a news program.

The AFO controls the media. Before Aspen woke up and learned to see through the brain washing, she believed everything that came out of the mouths of the news anchors. The first news story that comes across the TV is about the AFO securing a smaller country from a threat on the other side of the globe. The AFO is always engaging in conflicts outside of the country to influence their way of thinking. People enjoy being the heroes.

The door to the bathroom opens up and Oscar steps out in a towel before walking to the bedroom. Vex stands up and walks to the bathroom to take a shower now that Oscar is done. When Oscar is dressed, he walks over to the couch and kneels down near her leg and takes a drink of water from the water bottle.

"How are you feeling?" Doctor Oscar asks as he feels and looks at Aspen's wound.

"Good. Little sore," Aspen responds.

He removes the outside bandage which has little blood, which is good. Oscar then starts taking off the inner bandages which look good as well. He looks over the wound and thoroughly checks it over. Once Oscar feels good about it, he rewraps Aspen's leg and walks to the kitchen.

Oscar walks out of the kitchen with a few muffins that he hands to Jared and Aspen. Vex comes out of the bathroom and goes to the bedroom to change. The group always keeps extra clothes at safe houses. As everyone eats their muffins and chit chats, Vex comes out of the bedroom, hair still moist and grabs a muffin from Oscar.

"There's no more hot water," Vex says as he stuffs the muffin her mouth.

"I could use a shower. Hot or cold," Aspen says.

"Just don't get your leg wet," Oscar says.

"Never mind then."

Jared sits up near the front of the recliner and lights up another cigarette.

"We have the blueprints for the Mimir. Now we just need the bot that is posing as Aspen so we can broadcast them to the world together."

"So... at the Mimir we can message the whole world?" Aspen asks.

"That's what our mole at the NSA tells me," Jared replies.

"Speaking of our mole Jared. I tried messaging him to get information on you guys but he never responded," Oscar says.

"He won't reply to any message, Oscar. It has to be in a decrypt code," Jared says. "We need to go to Aspen's house and remove the bot. Hopefully alive, but it doesn't matter. Our message will get across either way."

"My husband is there. My kids are there. Jared... you make this sound like we're going in guns blazing."

"Aspen... there is no fucking way that your house and family is not being watched. They will shoot us; they will kill us. We need to kill them first. Got it," Vex says.

"Our mole might be able to give me the security details so we can get in and out. Hopefully with no deaths on our side."

Scenarios start to run through Aspen's head of losing any members of her family. She is scared and cannot the thoughts out of her head.

"Oscar; I have a special mission for you," Jared says.

“What is it?”

“I need you to get the word out to our other groups in the cities around us. We will need their help to get into the Mimir.”

“Ok…” Oscar replies.

“Go now. Meet at the old beer warehouse in Lake Rotchel in two days. Have everyone pass the word.”

“Why don’t you just message them?”

“Make them feel your urgency and understand the impact this will have for the fight. Tell them everything that has happened with Aspen and to our team,” Jared says as he stands up. “In two days, on the second night; we plan the downfall of the AFO.”

“Let’s do it,” Oscar says as he stands up and hugs Jared.

Oscar goes to the bedroom and comes out with a bag of clothes. He gives everyone a hug before he leaves and instructs Vex on how to rewrap Aspen’s leg. He waves goodbye as he steps out the door, closing it behind him.

“How many people are in the ANA?” Aspen asks.

“I don’t know; a lot,” Jared says. “Hundreds maybe.”

“Let’s talk about Aspen’s house,” Vex says.

“We go tonight. Me and you,” Jared says. “Aspen; you stay here.”

Aspen; upset at the thought of not going to rescue her family, tries to stand up but irks in pain before falling down onto the couch.

"I'll do everything I can to get your family ok," Vex says as she sits next to Aspen.

"And we will have a greater chance of saving your family if it's just the two of us. You're not ready for this."

After a bout of arguing, Aspen agrees she should stay behind and lays back down on the couch with the help of Vex.

"I'm going to reach out to our mole. See if they can give us the scoop on the security at your house. Maybe they can draw people away giving us an easier go at it," Jared says.

"Is the mole high up in the AFO that they could that?" Aspen asks.

"I don't know. I don't even know their real name."

÷

Thomas Harlow sits at the table in his house reading over the news on his tablet. Thomas is not rushing to the office today and decides to go in later. He wears a glossy gray set of glasses over his eyes to read as he drinks coffee out of his favorite mug. 'World's Best

Dad' is written in various colors across the face of the cup. It was given to him by his eldest daughter who is now on the verge of graduating high school. He is already dressed in his suit minus his coat, which he has draped over the chair he is sitting on

As he drinks his coffee, a little boy runs into the kitchen and starts tugging at Thomas' shirt. He laughs and sets his tablet down to see his youngest son staring up at him and tugging. Thomas grabs his son and sits him on his lap. Thomas' wife comes in to grab the boy.

"It's okay honey. Little George just wants to see his daddy," Thomas says as his wife picks George off his lap.

Thomas' phone vibrates on the table as his wife leaves the kitchen. He looks at it for a second as it vibrates before he grabs it and looks at whose calling. It is the Senior Security Officer at the Mimir.

"What is it?" Harlow asks.

"Sir, I have something that you need to see."

"What is it?" Harlow says impatiently.

"I'd rather not say on the phone, sir. It's not safe."

"Ok… I'm on my way," Thomas says as he gulps down his coffee.

Harlow stands up and grabs his coat, which covers the large knife on his belt. He walks into the living room and gives his wife and child a kiss goodbye before he goes to the garage of his mansion and gets in his car. After he backs out and gets into the street he lives on, he sets his car to autonomous mode to head to the Mimir. The car travels down a well paved street through million-dollar homes until it reaches the gate of the housing community Harlow lives in.

The guard lets him pass and his car continues down winding roads and bustling communities until he reaches another gate. This gate is to allow him onto the interstate. Only the richest, most influential neighborhoods, often where political figures and business magnates live, have the communities gated off from outsiders. A pass is required to gain entry to certain entrances and exits. Once Harlow passes security, his car travels onto the interstate and brings him to the NSA complex. He switches his car into manual mode and pulls up to the side of the security gate where he is allowed in without getting checked.

Harlow drives down the road into the complex and passes the parking lots where everyone parks. He pulls around the buildings and ends up behind the Mimir in a small parking lot surrounded by trimmed hedges that block the lot from view. Harlow gets out of his car after he parks in his spot and walks along the path to the entrance of the Mimir. As he rides down the elevator, he checks his phone for the time. It is nearly noon and he needs a drink. The elevator arrives to the command center. Harlow walks directly to the security officer's office and opens the door.

"Come with me," Director Harlow says.

and tells him to come to his office. With the officer right behind him, Harlow walks across the command center and up the stairs to his office. He has the officer lock the door behind him.

"So... what is it?" Harlow asks as he starts mixing a drink.

"I think there is a mole. Here in the complex."

"A mole," Harlow says as he walks behind his desk and faces the manager. "Who is it?"

"I'm not sure exactly who it is, sir. My team intercepted this message from an unauthorized phone on the property before it went offline," the officer says as they slide a tablet across Harlow's desk containing the message.

"Interesting..." Harlow says as he looks at the message on the tablet. "Why did it take so long to catch this person?"

"Whoever this is, is using an aftermarket spoofing replicator. It's a chip that can be put into any phone. It allows them to use our towers without us being able to track it."

"So you have a message that can't be linked to anybody."

"Not exactly," the officer says as they slip a piece of paper across the desk to Harlow from their pocket. "This is the phones location when it pinged us."

Harlow reads the slip of paper. "You can go now. Leave the tablet here."

"Understood."

The officer stands up and leave the office. Harlow looks at the message on the tablet and at the piece of paper thinking that whoever the mole is cannot be so stupid. He thinks about it for a moment as he finishes his drink. Director Harlow grabs his phone and calls Agent Leadheim to request his assistance. He then calls Charlie to make sure every single analyst is in the building in exactly twenty minutes and to confiscate everyone's phone.

Director Harlow leaves his officer after putting on coat. From his officer and across the complex, Harlow stews over the questions in his head regarding the mole situation and finds himself becoming paranoid. He arrives out front of the building indicated on the note and waits for Agent Leadheim to arrive.

Once Leadheim arrives, Harlow fills him in on what is going on. Leadheim nods his head and the two walk into the building and take the elevator to bring them down. Harlow collects his composure right before the door opens into the command center. He steps out with a smile, followed by Leadheim. He walks toward Charlie who is sitting in his office. Every analyst looks around at each other wondering why Director Harlow is there. Charlie stands when Director Thomas Harlow approaches him. Once Harlow and Leadheim are in Charlie's office, Leadheim closes the door and closes the shades on the windows.

"Hello, sir," Charlie says as he shakes Harlow's hand.

"Did you collect everyone's phones?"

"Yes, sir. Except for one. Analyst number nine says he lost his phone. Lance Hiland is his name," Charlie says as he hands the bag of phones to Director Harlow.

"Is your phone in here as well," Harlow says as he shakes the bag.

"Now it is," Charlie says as he drops his phone in the bag. "What is this about, sir?"

"You'll find out. Let's go."

Leadheim opens the door from Charlie's office and lets Director Harlow and Charlie step out first before he closes the door. Harlow hands the bag of phones back to Charlie.

"Attention everyone. Please stand up and face the open aisle," Harlow announces.

Every analyst stands up out of their chairs and stands at near attention towards the main aisles. Some crack their knuckles while others make sure not to lock their knees. Harlow starts walking down one aisle, very slowly, and shadowed by Agent Leadheim.

"I have something to share with you all. There is a traitor among you. I know it comes as a shock to the loyal AFO supporters I see in this room. I am hoping this traitor does the right thing and comes forward now. Perhaps; if they provide me with information, I find useful, I will spare their life."

Director Harlow stops in the front of the room and looks around. He contemplates his next move and chooses his words carefully. Harlow continues up the other aisle towards analyst number nine.

"This is... disappointing. I was really hoping for a peaceful resolution to this," Harlow says as he stops near Lance Hiland, looking him in the eye.

"Don't you wish... there was a peaceful resolution to this problem?"

"Of-of course, sir."

"Then... speak!" Harlow yells into his face.

The analyst, Lance Hiland cannot find the words to use after being accused and yelled at by Director Thomas Harlow.

Director Harlow looks over at Agent Leadheim and nods his head. Leadheim pulls out a black bag and shoves it over Lance's head and shoves him to the ground face first. He starts screaming through the bag as Leadheim binds his hands behind his back. Other analysts in the room gasp at the sight of the man being black-bagged. Mr. Hiland screams about his innocence in a muffled tone through the black bag. Leadheim gets him to his feet and pushes a gun up to his head. The room gets silent. All that can be heard is crying from Lance Hiland.

"Do not feel sorry for this man," Harlow says as he walks up to stand near Charlie. "Any man or woman that betrays me, is betraying you; and your families; and our country. They deserve to die. Don't you agree Charlie?"

"Of course, sir," Charlie says.

"Good. Let's go Agent Leadheim," Harlow says as he starts walking toward the elevator.

Harlow gets on the elevator followed by Leadheim and the black-bagged Mr. Hiland. All the analysts remain standing, still shocked at what they had just witnessed.

"Everybody get back to work. Let's go," Charlie says as he claps his hand. "We have a search to continue."

The analysts quickly sit down and begin working. Charlie goes in his office, closes the door, and sits down at his desk as he sets the bag of phones down on is desk.

The elevator reaches the ground level and Director Harlow exits the elevator with Leadheim and Lance Hiland right behind him.

"Bring him to the Roq. I'll meet you there," Harlow says as people look on.

Mr. Hiland starts to freak out and tries to get away from Leadheim's grasp at the mention of the Roq. This angers Leadheim, so he puts his arm around the man's throat and forces him toward a vehicle that is parked nearby. Some men get out and assist Leadheim in getting Lance into the back. Leadheim gets in the front seat and they drive away. Director Harlow continues walking across the complex toward the Mimir and his car, without looking back.

Harlow gets in his car and starts driving out of the complex. When he exits the security gate, he puts his car in autonomous mode. Harlow continues to fascinate about the mole situation and tries to make sense of it all. He is not confident that he has the correct person, but he hopes that he least scared the the room. Fear is a powerful deterrent.

Harlow grabs the wheel once he nears the Roq. He shows his ID and gets directed in by the guards. Harlow drives his car into the warehouse and takes the elevator down where he sees the vehicle that Leadheim was in with Mr. Lance Hiland. He parks next to it, grabs a pair of gloves out of the console, and gets out to soldiers standing at attention. The soldiers salute Harlow and welcome him to the Roq.

"Where is Agent Leadheim?" Harlow asks the commanding officer.

"Room nine, sir."

"Good. At ease."

Director Harlow walks down the long white hallway passing room after room until he reaches door number nine. He opens the door and slowly closes it behind him. At the center of the room is the analyst, Lance Hiland, tied to a chair and stripped down to his underwear. Leadheim hovers over the top of the analyst who has urinated on the floor. Harlow unbuttons his coat as he walks across the room and throws it off to the side. He then pulls out the pair of gloves from his right pocket. As Harlow slides them over his hand, Lance pleads for his life.

"Please. I… I don't know why I'm here," Lance begs.

Leadheim hits Lance across the face.

"You will speak when you are spoken to," Leadheim says.

Once Harlow gets the gloves on tight, he rolls up his sleeves and steps in front of the analyst.

"You don't look right," Harlow says as he reaches to his side and unsheathes a large knife. The blade is extremely sharp with a serrated edge along the top. "Being a traitor deserves the traitor scratch."

Harlow steps forward and grabs Lance by the hair, pulling his head back. He makes a deep slice across his left cheek, branding him as a Citizen 3. Lance yells in pain as blood drips off his face.

"Tell me what I want to know," Harlow says.

Lance continues to scream in pain.

"The messages. The ANA. You're a villain."

"Wha-what messages?"

"You know. I think I believe you," Harlow says as he walks up to Lance. "But I'm still going to kill you."

Harlow slides his knife across the throat of Lance Hiland and then walks away.

“This guy is a fall guy. Someone else in that room is responsible and we need to find out who. Go to Mr. Hiland’s home and find that phone,” Harlow says as he removes his gloves and throws them on the floor.

“Yes, sir.”

Harlow, followed closely by Agent Leadheim, grabs his coat and walks out the door as Lance’s life ceases to exist. Harlow goes into the bathroom to clean his knife. He runs it through the water at the sink, washing the blood off and dries the blade on his shirt. Harlow walks out of the bathroom and sheathes his blade as he walks.

“Clean up the room,” Director Thomas Harlow says to the soldiers as he gets into his car. “Dispose of everything.”

÷

Agent Leadheim drives out of the Roq and heads toward the house of Lance Hiland. He arrives there in the afternoon. It is a townhouse complex. Each townhouse has two floors and has an apartment underneath. Leadheim pulls up to the third building and parks in the parking lot toward the back of the building. He walks to unit number four, which is facing the street. He walks up a set of steps and holds onto the wrought iron rail as he approaches the door. Leadheim looks down at a welcome mat with a picture of a dog and the words ‘woof woof woof’ emblazoned on it.

Leadheim looks side to side to see if anyone is watching him. He reaches into his coat and begins to pull out Lance’s name tag until her hears a voice behind him. He quickly puts it away and turns around.

“I said… can I help you with something?” asks a girl with short hair wearing a green shirt and a green baseball cap.

“No. Just grabbing something for Lance.”

“You work with him or something?”

“Yes, I do. We’re good friends at the office.”

“Sure, you are.”

“Is that Lance’s dog? Talks about him all the time,” Leadheim says as he walks down the steps and toward the girl.

“Sassy is a girl. Not a boy”

“Right. Why do you have her?” Leadheim asks as he looks around.

“Look at the hat and the t-shirt. 3P; Pro Pet People. We take care of your pets so you don’t have too,” the girls says as she points out the logo and motto on her shirt and hat which are written on in permanent marker.

“Right. I’m going to go grab that stuff for Lance,” Leadheim says as he holds Lance’s name tag up in the air and walks up to the door.

“Ok, but tell Lance he owes me double because Sassy been throwing up.”

“I’ll let him know,” Leadheim says as he slides the name tag and slips inside the building, quickly shutting the door behind him.

Leadheim puts both hands on the door and looks through the peephole to see what the girl does. She looks around and at the door for a second before she turns around and walks down the sidewalk with Sassy in tow to continue the dog walk.

Once the girl is out of view, Leadheim turns around and looks into the townhouse. To the left are stairs leading upstairs and to the right is the living room. He goes to the right first and past the couch and coffee table, which had a few magazines on it about video games and other tech. Against the wall is Lance’s computer, which he starts up. Upon seeing a password lock, he shuts the computer down and continues toward the kitchen in the back of the home. He walks by the kitchen table where Lance has a few bills sitting out ready to be paid and peeks into the kitchen.

Finding nothing on the main floor is frustrating for Leadheim, but he continues on upstairs to the second floor. Upstairs is a small bathroom that Leadheim peaks into. There are also two rooms. Leadheim starts with the empty room which has clothes hanging and small totes of things on a shelf up above. He starts ripping down the totes and boxes, tearing through papers and memorabilia that are stacked up there. With no results in the empty room, he goes into the bedroom and starts rifling through the nightstand. After finding nothing, Leadheim flips the mattress; then flips the box spring; finding nothing.

Leadheim gets frustrated as he leaves the bedroom and heads downstairs. Once there, he flips the couch and kitchen table. Then he starts ripping everything out of the kitchen cabinets; finding nothing. Leadheim, with the feeling of defeat, goes and sits down on the computer chair in front of Lance's computer. As he sits, Leadheim looks around and thinks.

Suddenly the door-bell rings, prompting Leadheim to pull his pistol hastily from inside his coat. He walks slowly over to the door as it rings again. Once he reaches the door, Leadheim looks through the peephole to see two police officers. One standing next to the door and the other near the street; with the girl from earlier. Leadheim slides his gun back into its holster and pulls out his AFO badge before he opens the door.

"Hello officers," Leadheim says as he holds up his badge.

"Oh. Sorry about that sir. Kid here thought you were a thief. Continue on... whatever you're doing," says the officer before he starts walking down the steps.

"He is with the AFO little girl. Everything is alright," the officer says to the girl.

"But Lance never has anyone come to his house and now he has two visitors in two days," the girl says to the officers.

This catches Leadheim's ear as he starts to walk back into the townhouse. He immediately turns around and begins to walk toward the girl and the officers.

"You know; that's why I am. I'm trying to find out who the person was that visited Lance the other day," Leadheim says as he approaches the girl.

"He just walked in with Lance's card while I was feeding Sassy. He said the same thing you did. He's Lance's friend yada yada yada."

"What did he want? What did he look like?" Leadheim asks.

"I don't know; I left shortly after. He wasn't as creepy as you are."

"Did he give you a name?"

"Did you?" the girl says back with attitude.

Agent Leadheim turns away from the girl and walks back to the townhouse while the police talk with the girl. He steps over the welcome mat after looking at it and goes inside into the living room. He looks around at the pictures on the wall and the furniture tipped over and thinks. He starts to dig deeper into the home, cutting open the sofa and pulling appliances from the walls. When he goes upstairs, he searches through the bathroom vanity and toilet before cutting the mattress open.

As Leadheim is cutting open the mattress, he spots a dog bed out of the corner of his eye at the end of the room. He walks over and picks it up, only to see nothing underneath. Then he notices a slip cut underneath the bottom ring of the dog bed. Leadheim slowly slides his hand into the cut and feels a solid object. He clamps his hand around it and pulls out a cell phone. He starts it up and is immediately greeted with a password lock. Leadheim puts the phone to sleep and puts it in his pocket as he leaves the room. He exits the townhouse and heads back to the office, where someone can crack the password and any other possible encryption on the device.

÷

As the day turns to night, Vex and Jared leaves the apartment. They take the vehicle they took from Needham and ditch it, stealing another car in the process. Vex drives while Jared lays down in the backseat. After looking at a map Aspen drew for them, Vex and Jared decide to park at a nature preserve nearby and take the walking trails, which can be accessed from her house.

As Vex approaches the parking lot, she turns off the lights to the car and drives dark, using the streetlights as a guide. Vex turns into the parking lot and lightly uses the accelerator to make as little noise as possible. She parks away from any light so they are not detected. As soon as they park, they get out of the car and start walking towards Aspen's house with rifles in hand. Once they can see the house clearly, they get down on their bellies and watch.

The motion light on the back of the house is permanently on, allowing Vex and Jared to see at least two guards watching the patio doors in the back. They keep watching to see if anyone is patrolling the backyard, but after thirty minutes they don't see a soul. The only light on in the house is the light in the kitchen; the rest of the house is dark. All the bedrooms are upstairs, so the goal is to run in, grab everyone hopefully without much resistance, and get out as fast as possible. The only real concern they have is dealing with Aspen's husband Nolan and the bot. The kids can be grabbed easily without much effort.

Jared motions for them to move forward as they both start inching their way to the small path leading into Aspen's backyard. They move slowly, making sure to avoid stepping on branches and twigs in the path. They get near the shed in the backyard without being seen. From this point on, Jared and Vex know that they have to shoot and run. The equipment they have is not adequate for a nighttime rescue operation.

Vex thinks about luring a guard away, but can't know for certain if one or both guards would come; or if they would call it in. Jared wants to sneak up and knife them quietly, but if the guards have night-vision they wouldn't be able to get that close. Both felt lucky that they even made it to the shed without being detected. The safest plan to surprise them. Jared says he is going to take out the guard on the deck and go through the patio door there. Vex will kill the guard on the patio below and go through the patio door there.

"Let's do this," Jared whispers.

"Three…"

"Two…"

"One…"

"Go," Jared whispers.

Jared goes out first pushing his feet deep into the ground to accelerate quickly. He is followed closely by Vex who follows right on his tail. Before the guards understand what is going on; Jared starts firing his rifle, killing the guard and sending bullets through the patio door on the deck. Vex begins to fire almost in sync with Jared as she kills the guard sending him down hard onto the concrete. She runs full speed toward the patio door, firing more bullets into it to weaken the glass. Vex jumps through, back first, as Jared climbs the steps of the deck.

Once Vex is inside she turns her gun towards the staircase and fires at a guard who she sees running upstairs towards the bedroom. Another guard rushes up by the staircase and starts firing at Vex, who dashes across the living room, jumping behind a couch for cover. She yells for Jared to start firing through the patio door, which he does before jumping through, and kills the guard. They can hear the children cry and scream as Jared pushes out the glass with his foot as he steps into the house. Vex runs up the steps as Jared fires and shoots a guard who runs up to the front door.

"Jared! There's a guard upstairs!" Vex yells, prompting Jared to aim upstairs.

"I'll go up there. Stay here and cover."

"You got it."

Jared points his rifle upstairs as he slowly walks up the stairs. Vex positions herself behind the stair railing and fires at the other guards that she sees running up to the front door. The guards use the cover to the sides of the door and fire back as Vex gets involved in a firefight.

The bullets flying below him seem silent as he walks slowly down the hallway toward the bedrooms upstairs. Jared hears crying and screaming as he tiptoes past the bathroom. The hardwood floors creak as he walks.

"Don't come any closer or I will kill everyone in this room. You understand me!" yells out Agent F.

Nolan and Claudia are taken aback. Jared stops walking immediately after the guard calls him out.

"You don't have to do that man!" Jared yells back over the gunfire from downstairs. "You don't want to kill those kids!"

"Don't test me."

Jared needs to make a decision, and he needs to make it quickly. Does he continue to try and negotiate with the threatening agent or does he make a dash for the bedroom.

Due to his past experiences in dealing with agents of the AFO, Jared makes the decision to rush forward. He is five steps away from the doorway as he leaps forward. After his third step he hears gunfire coming from the room. As soon as Jared can see into the bedroom, he shoots the agent that is firing upon Aspen's family. When he looks down at Aspen's family, he sheds a tear.

Nolan, Claudia, and the kids are bloodied and full of bullets. All are dead except for Houston, who is gasping for air as blood splatters from his mouth. After a moment, he stops moving and passes on. Jared finds himself shaken as he blocks out everything and travels to memories from things he saw as a kid.

Jared can hear screams from Vex to hurry up as his brain starts to function. He grabs Claudia's leg, pulling her from the grasps of Nolan's lifeless body. Once he has her in the middle of the room, he kneels down and picks her body up, throwing it over his shoulder. Jared puts a pistol in one hand as he holds the legs of Claudia tight to his chest. He hustles as fast he can down the hallway toward the stairs.

"Cover me!" Jared yells.

Vex puts in her last clip and steps out from behind the stairwell and unloads her rifle at the doorway as

Jared slips by and downstairs. Vex follows behind as they step through the broken patio door to the concrete patio.

Jared starts running across the yard as Vex waits for the last guard to pursue them. Once the guard passes the staircase, Vex uses the last of her ammo to put them to the ground. She immediately turns around to run after Jared across the yard.

"Where's Aspens family?" Vex asks as they run on the trail toward the car.

"Their dead."

"What!"

"Let's just get the fuck out of here!" Jared yells.

Vex and Jared run across the parking lot to the car, where Jared puts Claudia's body in the trunk before getting laying down in the backseat. Vex gets in the driver's seat, puts the car into gear, hops a curb, and starts driving down the path into the nature preserve and away from Aspen's house.

÷

The phone keeps ringing until Director Harlow reaches over to his nightstand. He tips the phone up and sees that Charlie is calling him. Harlow pulls the phone off the wireless charger and swipes answer to speak with Charlie.

"What is it Charlie?"

"Director Harlow; ANA hit the James house."

Harlow immediately wakes up to the fullest as he whips the covers off of him and walks toward his closet.

"What's the status of Claudia and the family?"

"A team will be there in four minutes with helicopter support and I will have that answer for you."

"Where are you, Charlie?" Harlow asks as he finishes putting clothes on.

"In my car and on the way."

"Tell the guard it's a Code Forty-Six. He should let you in immediately. I'm almost in my car."

"Understood."

Director Harlow hangs up the phone as he hits the garage door button on the wall in the garage and gets in his car. He reverses rapidly out of the garage and quickly accelerates into the street, leaving the garage door wide open.

Charlie pulls up to the gate of the NSA complex, tells the guard the code, and is let in immediately. He speeds quickly through the trees and drives right up near the elevator, over the curb and everything. After he inputs his information into the elevator and makes his way down, he walks into the command center where the analysts are working ferociously to contain the situation.

He looks up at the screens and can see all the dead bodies scattered in the house through the responding team's body cameras. Blood, glass, and gun casings litter the floor.

"Where is Claudia?" Charlie asks.

"She's gone, sir."

"Where are they now!"

"Our response teams found tracks going through the nature preserve. They followed them but haven't found anything yet. We are reviewing camera footage now to see where they went."

"Find these pieces of shit!"

Charlie paces at the top of the room as he watches camera footage from both inside the house and the streets. He starts biting his fingernails. The elevator door opens and Director Harlow steps out quickly and walks toward Charlie, who is chomping away.

"Status."

"ANA busted into Aspen James' house and took Claudia. We are trying to track the car they used get away. The husband Nolan and both children, Aiden and Houston are dead. Agent F and every member of Team Epsilon are dead."

Director Thomas Harlow, visibly upset, places both hands on the railing and leans down, stretching out his back.

"Who is responsible for watching the house?" Harlow asks.

"I am, sir."

Harlow stands back up and turns to face Charlie.

"I am sick of the incompetence of this room. I want Claudia found now. Not three days from now. Right. Now. Do you understand me?"

"Yes sir."

Director Harlow leans close to Charlie to whisper into his ear.

"The next mistake from you and your team will result in your body on the floor," Director Harlow whispers to Charlie before he steps away and walks onto the elevator.

÷

Vex and Jared know the AFO is tracking the vehicle they drove out of the nature preserve and watching and cameras to see where they went. Unfortunately for the AFO, Vex and Jared know where they can switch vehicles without a camera catching them.

Switch sites is what they call them. It can be a parking lot with a broken camera or a neighborhood street that is away from the AFO's prying eyes. They always used switch sites at least twice to be sure they lose whoever is monitoring them. Since the switch sites change so often with the AFO fixing everything, they decide to go even safer by switching vehicles three times.

The first switch they do is at an apartment complex with a known blind spot. The second switch occurs a few miles away at an overflow parking lot for factory employees. While it did have street cameras that could see it was poorly lit. The last switch site they went to was a street only ten blocks from the safe house. The people that live on the street are notorious for busting the cameras so often that the AFO does not replace them anymore.

Even with all three switches, Jared still feels that they need to leave the safe house and find refuge in the forest. Vex agrees, but tells Jared they need to give some time to Aspen before they leave. They both decide to give themselves until morning.

Jared sits back in the passenger seat once he parks as he tries to figure out what to say to Aspen. He lights up a cigarette as he thinks and takes long drags off the cigarette. Jared knows the emotion of loss all too well, especially when it comes to family. After he finishes his cigarette, he lights up another one immediately after. Vex tries to say something, but Jared stops her. When he finishes his second cigarette, he opens the door and gets out, along with Vex. They decide to leave Claudia's body in the car.

The steps moan and creak as they walk up the steps dragging their feet. Jared reaches the door first and breathes in deeply before looking at Vex, who simply nods. He turns the knob and slides through the door followed shortly after by Vex. Aspen is standing next to couch with her bum leg.

"Where's Nolan? Where are my children?" Aspen asks as her smile slides away once Vex closes the door.

The faces on both Jared and Vex tell the story Aspen does not want to hear. Her face goes from smiling to utter tragic in mere moments as tears start to slowly come from her eyes. The bulge in her face grows larger as she tries to contain herself from crying out loud. She cannot hold it any longer as she bursts out in sadness and anger.

"Where are they!" Aspen yells out.

"Aspen," Jared says quietly as he starts slowly walking toward her. "I'm so sorry..."

"Don't you say sorry to me you... fucker. Where is my family!" Aspen screams as she runs at Jared to attack him.

Jared rushes over with Vex to grab Aspen as she flails her arms around in anger at them. Jared grabs her and places his hand over her mouth to keep her quiet. They finally wrestle her down to the couch as she sobs, cries, and fights loudly over her family through Jared's hand.

Chapter 10

Director Harlow changes into clothes that he keeps in his office for emergencies. As he finishes changing and throws on a sport coat, someone knocks at his door and comes in.

"Good morning, Agent Leadheim"

"Good morning, Sir. I have something you need to see."

"What is it?" Director Harlow asks as he pours himself a drink.

"I had an analyst hack into and decrypt the phone I found at Mr. Buchman's home," Leadheim says as he pulls the phone out of his coat pocket and places it on Director Harlow's desk.

"What did you find?"

"Our friend was telling someone in the ANA about everything. Including everything to do with the Judas Project."

"Of course, he was, but I know that he was a simple patsy to the real traitor. Mr. Buchman was set up to fall right into our hands, just like the phone was. It was too easy," Harlow says as he looks out over the control room; circling his drink. "I want you to watch Charlie."

"Yes, Sir."

Agent Leadheim nods his head indicating his understanding of Director Harlow's order. He takes a step back before turning around and exiting the room. Harlow finishes his drink and sits down, opening the phone. There are multiple messages in different files that he reads over. Most messages are about the Judas Project and about the layout of the NSA complex. There are also messages about the doppel incident regarding Aspen and Claudia. There was a message sent immediately after the discovery of the doppel.

Director Harlow makes himself upset as he takes his keyboard and slides it off his desk violently. He stands up, breathing heavily, then starts grabbing and throwing things off his desk a fit of rage. Harlow, after his tantrum, collects himself and mixes another drink.

÷

Jared slowly opens his eyes as he wakes up laying crooked on the couch. He swings his legs over to the floor and yawns as he stretches his arms into the air. Jared looks around the room and turns his head around to look back into the bedroom and bathroom. No one else is awake yet. He stands up and walks slowly to the bathroom rubbing his eyes. When Jared walks into the bathroom, he discovers an awake and depressed Aspen sitting curled up in the shower.

Aspen slowly moves her eyes to look up at Jared for a brief second before putting her eyes back down. She has her knees up to her chin and her arms wrapped around her legs like she is hugging them. Pain is in her eyes.

"I know it hurts. I know the vengeful feeling you're going through. You want revenge and it's understandable," Jared says as he kneels down in front of Aspen. "Remember that there is no sympathy. There is only revolution."

Aspen starts breathing heavily and lunges at Jared, toppling him over and landing on top of him. She tries to grab Jared by the throat, but he is too strong. Jared can see the hatred in her eyes as she hits and slaps him. Jared does his best not to hurt her.

"You killed my family you piece of shit! It is your fault they are dead!" Aspen screams at the top of her lungs as she hits Jared.

Vex, who wakes up to the commotion, runs into the bathroom.

"What the fuck is going on?" Vex asks as she grabs hold of Aspen and pulls her off Jared.

"You're a murderer!" Aspen yells.

Vex finally wrestles control of Aspen in the living room before Aspen falls to her knees crying with both hands over her face. Jared and Vex simply look at each other as Aspen cries. After second seconds or so, Aspen removes her hands and looks at Jared who is still standing in the doorway to the bathroom. Her face is beat red and glistening wet. Her eyes are swollen from the rubbing and are barely open.

"You think you're some kind of hero… but you're not," Aspen says softly to Jared. "You're the AFO with a different name."

Aspen stands up slowly and slides her way toward the bedroom, staring at Jared the entire time. Vex and Jared lock eyes before Vex goes behind Aspen to help her to the bedroom. Jared, still taking everything in, stays silent. He walks over to the couch to sit down and reflect. He puts his elbows to knees and rests his head on his hands when he hears the door squeak close.

Jared struggles mentally on whether or not he is truly the villain. He lights up a cigarette and takes deep drags.

Twenty minutes later and three cigarettes Jared hears the door to the bedroom creak open. Jared turns his head around to look over the couch. He sees Vex step out quietly into the hallway before closing the door behind her. Vex tip-toes slowly into the living room while wiping away dried tears on her cheeks. She sits down on the recliner.

"How is she?" Jared whispers.

"She is calm now. She didn't sleep last night. No surprise."

"We need to leave. Like we agreed."

"I know."

An awkward silence ensues for a minute before Vex decides to speak out.

"Did you kill that family in Needham? Aspen says she saw a bunch of blood on your hands when we got here that night."

"I didn't want to risk them getting free and exposing us. It's better this way."

"You do realize that you give the AFO ammunition for their propaganda when you do that right?" Vex whispers. "And they aren't lying when they say we did it. No wonder people hate us; we are monsters."

"Those people were brainwashed in Needham. Basically everyone is," Jared whispers as he lights up another cigarette.

"So are you, Jared," Vex says angrily while pointing at Jared. "So are you."

"Fuck you."

"You're a child," Vex says as she stands up. "That family was innocent. With the right information they would understand why we do what we do. Everyone can. Got it."

Vex walks away to the bedroom.

"We'll be ready soon," Vex says as she closes the door.

Jared puts his head in his hands and shuts them. He separates himself from the world and brings himself back to a simpler time; with his mother.

Half an hour goes by and Jared hears the door open from the bedroom. He stands up immediately to see Aspen wrapped in a blanket hovered by Vex. They slowly walk down the hallway toward Jared and then toward to the bathroom. Aspen keeps her eyes on the floor and walks with zero life.

"Grab the bags Jared," Vex says.

Jared walks to the bedroom without saying a word as Vex closes the bathroom door; locking herself and Aspen inside. Vex opens the door on the vanity below the sink and pulls out a shaver. She looks at Aspen and runs her hand through Aspen's blonde hair. Vex turns around and leans up against the vanity to face Aspen, who is glaring into the mirror.

"Want me to do it? Or are you?" Vex asks Aspen as she starts up the shaver.

"Do we have too?"

"You are one of the most wanted people in the city. Maybe the country."

"Are you shaving your hair off too?"

"Sure," Vex says as she turns around and starts shaving the hair off her head."

Vex hardly has much hair on her head. She has cut and shaved her head quite a few times. Once Vex is done, she turns off the shaver and hands it to Aspen.

"What does it feel like?"

"It's cooler."

Aspen looks herself in the mirror and runs her left hand through her hair one last time before she starts shaving it off. She starts slow as she rounds over the top of her head, progressively gets faster the more times she runs it through. Blonde locks of hair fall into the sink and bounce off her shoulders as they float to the floor. When Aspen is done, she turns off the shaver and drops it in the sink. She runs both her hands over her prickly shaved head.

"You're still beautiful. Remember that," Vex whispers to Aspen as she opens the door. "Let's go."

Aspen wraps the blanket around herself as they exit the bathroom to find Jared standing at the door waiting for them.

"Ready to go?" Jared says to zero acknowledgement by Aspen.

They all exit the apartment and walk down the steps and into the lobby before going into the alleyway. Jared gets in the backseat and lays down, while Aspen sits in the front seat with Vex driving. Once they are all comfortably inside, Vex drives to the end of the alley, looks both ways, and turns into the street.

"How many switch sites you figure we need to stop at Jared?"

"Four in my honest opinion."

After the last switch at the garage, Vex takes their newly acquired vehicle into the forest to the west of the city to hide out. Their plan is to drive as far in as they can, just off the beaten path, and hide the vehicle. From there, they will hike to another hidden cave system to wait until the night of the meeting.

÷

Through a window across from Charlie's apartment, Agent Leadheim sits in a metal folding chair. With his binoculars he watches Charlie prepare for his day. Charlie wakes up, takes a shower, and gets dressed in a blue suit with a blue tie. As he eats breakfast, Leadheim observes him messaging on his phone. Unfortunately, the phone is at an odd angle, not allowing Leadheim to read the messages. Once Charlie is finished eating, he puts his dishes in the sink, grabs his briefcase, and exits his apartment, locking it behind him.

Agent Leadheim makes note of the time so he can check messages being sent and received in that building. He stands up and looks down until he can see Charlie's car drive down the street. As the car turns and exits out of view, Leadheim buttons his coat and sets the binoculars down on the chair he was sitting in. He walks towards the door to the apartment and walks by the body of an old man in the living room with blood pooled in front his chest; seeping into the carpet.

"Thank you," Leadheim says to the old man he stabbed to death before he walks out the door, locking it behind him.

The walk to the elevator is long, as Leadheim makes his way down one apartment building only to traverse into another. Once he makes it down to the ground floor, he strolls out the front door and crosses the street without using a cross walk. Leadheim steps through the carousel front door and steps into a lobby full of staff and security. He approaches the guard near the elevator.

"I'm here to see a friend," Leadheim says to the guard as he shows his AFO badge.

The guard smirks and lets Agent Leadheim onto the elevator. After he hits the button to go to Charlie's floor, Leadheim stands and waits with his hands behind his back.

The elevator makes it to the bottom floor with a ding. Once the people vacate the lone elevator, Leadheim steps on and hits the button to go to Charlie's floor. As the door shuts, Leadheim sees two women rushing to the elevator yelling for him to hold the door, Leadheim allows the door to close in their faces.

When Leadheim arrives on the floor that Charlie's apartment is on, he steps out slowly looking both directions. He steps forward and starts walking down the long hallway to Charlie's apartment door. Leadheim keeps his eyes and ears open, ready to attack at any moment. At the near end of the long hallway, Agent Leadheim turns to look at the door. He reaches into his pocket and pulls out a magnetic stripped card to swipe into the card reader to unlock the door. Once it is in the lock, it takes a second to hack into the lock, forcing it to open.

The lock turns, giving Leadheim access to Charlie's apartment. He takes the card and slides it back into his pocket before grabbing the door handle and walking in. Once inside, he closes the door and steps forward. Agent Leadheim exits the entryway immediately and walks into the living room. He decides to start in the bedroom and walks behind the couch before walking into the bedroom.

Leadheim starts opening drawers on the dresser and nightstand, looking for anything that could incriminate Charlie. After finding nothing there, Leadheim looks under the bed and the pillows, but still finds nothing. After finding nothing in the bedroom, he moves on and goes through the bathroom next; then the living room, dining room, and kitchen. The lack of finding anything infuriates Agent Leadheim. He decides to leave the apartment and look up records on Charlie instead.

÷

Director Harlow, with a drink in one hand and his head in another, looks out across the control room; his kingdom, his empire. He is threatened and he can feel it. He built the NSA to where it is now and helped the AFO to become the leader it is, as a Senior Party Member.

Harlow starts to pace in his office as he thinks and conspires about an attack that may or may not happen. The paranoia grips him as he becomes convinced people in the building are working against him. All of this, everything, he thinks and feels; he keeps internalized. Nothing translates to his facial emotions or body language.

The whiskey in his cup is nearly gone, so Harlow finishes it in a gulp before he sits down and picks up his phone. He puts the phone up to his ear and pauses for a moment before he hits the speed dial. It starts to ring. After four rings, someone answers the phone in a deep, calming voice.

"Yes, Thomas."

"Tarrick. We are going to get attacked by the ANA."

"Are you sure?"

"Not 100%, but it feels like you said it would. In the city."

"What about the doppel situation? You haven't updated me with that?"

"It's handled. Everything else will be to."

"Good. It's a wonderful sacrifice what you're doing down their Thomas. I know it's a lot of hard work and long hours, but... you deserve it. You are doing your party proud. The AFO thanks you."

"Thank you, Sir."

After he hangs up the phone, Director Harlow stands up immediately and walks over to get a drink at his liquor cabinet.

÷

Jared hops over a fallen tree and cements his feet into unsuspecting mud.

"Watch your step here. Shits muddy."

He steps out of the mud and stops to light up a cigarette. Vex finds a way around the mud with Aspen behind her, trying to keep her distance from Jared. They continue walking together across the green forest untouched by modern man.

"We're close, but the sun doesn't wait for anyone," Jared says as he continues walking.

The group comes across a giant boulder covered in moss. Jared knows he is close to the cave system as he steps around the boulder and looks into the wall of rock that stands behind it. Jared starts to pull moss and vines off the back side of the rock, finally revealing a small entrance into cliff face.

The entrance to the cave is tight as Jared goes first to make sure everything is safe. He turns on the light on his gun squeezes through and disappears into the darkness. The sound of footsteps dissipates.

"Your good to come in! It's tight but it gets larger!" Jared yells out.

Aspen goes into the cave next, followed by Vex, who pushes the moss and vines back to cover the entrance. Aspen makes it to Jared and looks at him with the same disdain as before. Vex squeezes through the last stretch and steps into a larger cave body. Jared moves forward with a light with Aspen and Vex following him. The memories of the cave system start to slowly come back, for better or worse, as Jared walks.

With Jared leading the way, followed closely by Aspen and Vex, they make their way deeper into the caves. They cross a small stream before Jared stops and points his light at the wall. The words that are spray painted on the walls say 'Fuck the AFO' and 'Welcome Traitors'. They continue on and pass more writing on the walls before they start to come across various household items.

They step over things like broken plastic totes, kitchen ware, and blankets. It isn't long until Aspen spots a skeleton dressed up in military style gear with an old gun held tightly to its ribcage. It isn't long after they see the first skeleton that they start to see more.

Eventually the trio comes upon the remains of a gate structure made of wood and rock. Painted on a piece of wood attached to this gate is the word; Liberty.

"Jared… What is this place?" Vex asks.

"This is Liberty. The stronghold of the resistance at one point. Until it wasn't."

"What happened?" Vex asks.

"AFO found it. Killed everyone."

"If the AFO knows about this place, why would we come here?" Vex asks with her voice raised.

"They don't think about this place anymore… they don't want to," Jared says.

Jared steps through the gate to Liberty followed closely by Vex and Aspen. They come across more skeletons along with bullet casings everywhere across the cave. Eventually the cave opens up into a very large open area, the heart of Liberty. They walk slowly, shining their flashlights around the room; turning in circles. They see torn cloth and wood from the remains of small houses or shops in rubble around the room. A small waterfall from up above forms a small river and lake from erosion. Suddenly, Jared stops in his tracks. His breathing becomes erratic.

In front of them is a pile of skeletal remains. From adult remains down to children, the pile represents all that is horrible about the AFO. Jared reaches over his heart as he does his best to hold back any sort of tear.

He looks down toward the stone floor as he does his best to relax his breathing. He moves the light from his flashlight up to the wall, where 'No Sympathy, Only Revolution' is spray-painted across the wall.

"What happened here Jared?" Vex asks.

"I lived here. With my mother and lots of others who were fighting against the AFO. She established Liberty and remained the leader of the rebels. There were little shops and makeshift homes placed everywhere in this room. More people lived in and around the tunnels leading to here; including my mother and I. One day, Liberty was found and attacked by the AFO. The rebels fought hard to keep them from getting to the heart of Liberty, but they were overwhelmed and outgunned. When the AFO had killed all the people resisting; they gathered everyone that was still alive. Right here. The men, the women, and the children; right here. The only people not in the group was my mother and I. The AFO forced her to watch them kill everyone, one by one. They took knives and stabbed them in the throats. Once everyone was dead, they slit my mother's throat; in front of me. I remember her gasps for air as I tried to push away from the men that were holding me. As my mother, Ana, lay there lifeless in front of me, one of the AFO leaders took out his knife and slashed my cheek. After that they all left. Leaving me here to die. I bet they thought I would sit there and rot. But I came out of there with hatred. Hatred that has helped keep me alive. I left Liberty... and never came back. Until now..."

"Holy shit. Fuck them, Jared. Fuck 'em," Vex says.

"Yeah," Jared says as he lights up a cigarette. "Follow me."

Jared starts walking around the pile of skeletons, followed closely by Vex and Aspen, who both have tears in their eyes. He leads them to the back of the big room and into a smaller tunnel. They walk through this for a bit, passing sleeping bags, blankets, and pillows. Aspen spots numerous stuffed animals that start pulling on her emotions as they walk. Eventually they squeeze into a small offshoot in the tunnel that leads into a small room. There is blankets and some toys inside.

"Was this your room?" Aspen asks.

"Yeah. Let's grab some pillows and blankets from the corridor and get some rest."

"Can I ask you something Jared?" Aspen asks.

"Not right now. Please," Jared says.

Vex leaves the room to grab some things for the group. When Vex returns, they all lay down to get some sleep after brushing dust off the bedding. Jared sleeps closest to the entrance of the room, with Vex splitting Aspen and Jared up.

After everyone turns off their flashlights, Aspen leaves hers on and faces the cold wall of the cave. She looks at drawings on the wall of stick people and animals, most likely drawn by Jared. Aspen draws a few tears from the drawings; reminiscing about the drawings of her children she had on her fridge. She turns off the flashlight after a moment to get some sleep.

Aspen wakes up a few hours later to the sound of someone walking through the cave. She sits up and notices Jared is no longer laying down and is gone. She stands up and decides to follow him, bringing her blanket with her for warmth in the cold caves, and her flashlight. Aspen slowly steps over Vex, who is in a deep sleep, and starts squeezing through the cave until she reaches the main cave corridor. She looks down the cave and sees Jared with a flashlight. Aspen waits until Jared is out of view before turning on her own flashlight and following him. When she arrives to the heart of Liberty, Jared is standing there waiting for her, pointing his flashlight into her eyes.

"Hard to sneak about in here. Everything echoes."

"Yeah."

"I couldn't sleep," Jared says as he shines his flashlight on the 'No Sympathy, Only Revolution' motto on the wall. "Just can't stop thinking about this."

Jared sits down and Aspen walks over to sit next to him. She shines her flashlight over the saying as well; overlapping it with Jared's light.

"I always thought I understood what it meant. Lately I don't think I do," Jared says.

"Sympathy makes you weak; vulnerable. It forces you to make decisions based on emotion. If you let yourself be overcome with emotion; you can't fight. No fight means no revolution."

"It also makes everyone hate you," Jared says.

"I don't hate you. You just... have no sympathy. You live a life being unable to have sympathy. It's not your fault. I know you didn't kill my family. The AFO did. I just needed to lash out."

There is a silence for a moment as Jared sits still looking at the wall. Aspen looks at him unabashed as she sees a glisten in his eyes followed by slow moving tears picking up dirt as they roll down his face.

Aspen scoots closer to Jared and puts her arm around him to comfort him.

"Sorry for being inconsiderate about the loss of your family," Jared says as he moves his head to look into Aspen's eyes.

"Yeah," Aspen says as tears come from her eyes.

"Yeah.

Jared turns his eyes back forward with Aspen. They both look at the cave wall together until they slowly fall asleep in the heart of Liberty.

Chapter 11

The following morning Vex wakes up to see that both Jared and Aspen are not there. She wraps herself up in a blanket and makes her way out of the room into the corridor. Using her flashlight to guide her way, Vex arrives into the heart of Liberty to see Jared and Aspen sleeping soundly in the center of the room.

Vex turns off her flashlight to avoid waking them up, but it is too late; Aspen turns her head to see Vex staring at her, followed shortly after by Jared. Light peeks through the top of the cave near the top of the waterfall, lighting up the room.

"I guess you've made up then," Vex says.

"I think we understand each other a bit better," Aspen replies as she looks back at Jared.

"We need to get ready to go. How's your leg?" Vex asks Aspen.

"Mostly fine."

"We need to meet up with my mole," Jared says as he stands up. "Their coming to the meeting."

"Sounds good," Aspen says as she stands up.

Aspen and Vex follow Jared out of the cave tunnels back to where they came in. They hike through the woods and get to the vehicle they stole by mid-afternoon. As Vex drives into town, with Jared and

Aspen laying in the backseat, Jared tries to message his mole. Jared waits until he has service to contact them.

÷

It's nearly three in the afternoon and Charlie is on his way up the elevator. He is done for the day and walks to his car, hoping to not be bothered all weekend. As he walks out to his car, he runs into Agent Leadheim, who is standing near the parking lot, directly in Charlie's path.

"How's it going?"

"It's uh... good. What do you need?" Charlie says as he continues walking

"Nothing," Leadheim says as Charlie walks by. "Have a good day."

"Thanks... you to," Charlie replies, skeptical of Leadheim's intent.

Charlie watches as Leadheim disappears behind the buildings as he finishes walking to his car. He places his briefcase in the backseat and sits in the car, waiting to see if Leadheim comes back out to the parking lot. When nothing happens, Charlie looks around before backing up his car and heading out of the complex. As Charlie drives away, he constantly looks in the rear-view mirror and back at the road, expecting to be followed. His paranoia runs high.

Charlie drives home the entire time with his eyes on his mirrors. He notices a car that he suspects is following him; a white car, tinted heavily. Charlie continues like normal, trying not to draw attention to himself. As he approaches his apartment building, he sees the white car turn off the road and out of view.

When Charlie gets home, he looks around at the all the buildings before entering the lobby of his apartment complex. He sees nothing. Once he gets on the elevator, he pulls out his phone and reads a message on his phone. Charlie decrypts the message and replies to the sender.

The elevator door opens and Charlie starts walking down the hallway toward his apartment. When he reaches his apartment door, he swipes his card and hesitates walking inside. His phone vibrates a couple times as Charlie opens the door and looks in his apartment from the hallway. Charlie quickly closes the door and opens his phone to see the message. After the message decrypts, Charlie sighs as he holds the phone up and replies. He slides the phone into his pocket and goes into his apartment; with caution.

When Charlie goes in, he walks slowly over to the windows and shuts all the curtains. After all the windows are blocked in the living room, Charlie goes to his bedroom and shuts the curtain in there. When his entire apartment is blocked from outside views, Charlie sits down on the end of his bed. With his head in his hands, Charlie thinks hard about how to shake the agent, whom he believes is Leadheim.

÷

Leadheim watches as Charlie blocks his view to the apartment. He sets down his binoculars and grabs his phone from his pocket. Leadheim calls the main control room in the Mimir.

"This is Analyst 11."

"This is Agent Leadheim; I need all calls and messages from the phone and the building you looked into earlier for me."

"Understood. Checking."

Leadheim watches the apartment intently as he waits for the analyst to respond.

"Agent Leadheim..."

"Yes."

"The phone in question, belonging to Charlie Graham Stipper, is not being used currently. Last message was this morning to his mother. No calls in the last three days."

"Any other activity from his apartment?"

"Nothing from him. If he is communicating; it's not from an issued phone."

"Got it. Keep me updated."

Agent Leadheim hangs up his phone and sits down in the chair he has set-up in front of the window. He grabs the binoculars off the floor and watches Charlie's windows; waiting for him to slip up.

As time goes by, Leadheim continues to watch Charlie's apartment with great intent. The binoculars dent into the skin around his eyes as he watches. He removes one hand from the binoculars when his phone starts to ring so he can pick it up and remain glued to Charlie's apartment. On the phone is the analyst from earlier that is tracking Charlie's calls and messages.

"Yes."

"Mr. Stipper messaged a woman named Clarissa Jane. Looks like they are meeting up for food and drinks in one hour."

"Where?"

"The Sly Raccoon. Bar and restaurant just outside of downtown."

"Who's the girl?"

"Nothing of interest in her profile. She is a Citizen 2. No issues."

"Have they messaged before?"

"They have not."

"Track her phone. Keep me updated."

Leadheim hangs up the phone and continues to watch Charlie's apartment. The sun starts to set and darkness rolls in. The lights turn off in Charlie's apartment starting with the bedroom and then the living room. Leadheim sets his binoculars down on the chair as he stands up before walking to the door. Agent Leadheim walks quickly to the elevator and to his car so he can follow Charlie to the restaurant. He calls the analyst as he gets in his car.

"Where is he?"

"He just pulled out of parking garage and is headed down 15th Street toward the restaurant."

"Where is the girl?" Leadheim asks as he pulls out onto the road.

"She is walking into the Sly Raccoon right now."

"Do you have visual?"

"She went through the back entrance. There isn't cameras there. All I have is her cellphone."

"What about inside the restaurant?"

"Checking. Hold on."

Leadheim continues driving and eventually sees Charlie's car five lengths ahead of him. Rain starts to mist lightly on the windshield as he drives down the street. Charlie turns into a parking lot across the street from the restaurant. Agent Leadheim pulls off to the side of the road looking for a spot to see into the restaurant. There is a shoe shop half a block from the restaurant across the street that Leadheim starts walking toward. The rain starts picking up from a mist to a drizzle.

"Agent Leadheim."

"Go."

"No cameras in the restaurant. Mr. Stipper sent a message asking what entrance she was at. Ms. Jane said she was in the rear entrance."

Leadheim walks through the door to the shoe shop and shows his AFO badge to the owners. He demands to be allowed upstairs and onto the roof. The owners oblige and show Leadheim the entrance to the roof through a hatch. Once he is on the roof, Leadheim looks out across the street to see Charlie jogging through traffic toward the Sly Raccoon.

"Mr. Stipper is going across the street to the restaurant now."

"I see him."

Charlie walks around the back of the restaurant toward the rear entrance and out of view of Leadheim.

"I don't have visual. Tell me what's going on."

"Mr. Stipper and Ms. Jane are next to each other in the building. Looks they are standing there near the rear entrance. Now they are moving further into the building, still near the back. They have stopped."

Five minutes goes by and the tracking on the phones still has not moved. Leadheim grows impatient.

“Any movement yet?”

“No sir.”

“I’m going to wait in my car. Let me know if they move.”

“Understood.”

Agent Leadheim climbs down the roof hatch and walks out of the shoe store. Once he gets in his car, he lays back in wait.

÷

The door flies open on a large SUV in the parking lot behind the Sly Raccoon. Charlie gets in and lays down on the floor. The door gets closed behind him. Vex gets in the driver’s seat and slowly drives away, turning onto the street and away from the restaurant. She drives as normally as possible to avoid suspicion.

“Keep an eye out for a white car,” Charlie says.

“Keep your head down. Got it.”

Charlie looks around and sees Jared and Aspen both laying down on seats in the back, out of view.

“I recognize you, Aspen. That means you’re Jared. I’m Charlie.”

"Good to meet you Charlie," Jared responds. "I'm putting a lot of faith in you. If you fuck me over, I will kill you. You understand me," Jared says.

"I understand. You won't have to worry about me."

"Good."

"No tails. We are in the clear. Heading to the warehouse now."

Vex turns around and heads toward the old beer warehouse.

"We have two hours; max, before we have to be back. After that I'm sure they'll grow very suspicious."

"Where did you put the cellphones?" Jared asks.

"Hid them under a table and put them on silent. Who's the girl? Carissa Jane."

Jared pulls out a purse and pulls out a driver's license belonging to Carissa Jane.

"I told her if she reports it stolen, I would kill her family."

"You're ruthless."

"I am determined. If my determination requires me to be ruthless... so be it."

Jared puts everything back in the purse and lays it down on the floor. Jared lays back his head.

"Wake me up when we get there," Jared says as he closes his eyes.

"Charlie?" Aspen asks.

"Yeah."

"Why are you doing this?"

"I've seen shit. A lot of shit," Charlie says as he looks at Aspen. "I am here to save my soul... at least what's left."

Vex pulls into a large industrial area on the banks of Lake Rotchel and drives by multiple warehouses before pulling up to the old beer warehouse with directions from Jared. Vex turns off her headlights before pulling into an open door. Once inside, she pulls up alongside multiple vehicles, including the van Oscar was driving.

Jared, followed by Aspen, Vex, and Charlie walk through the dark until they reach a small lit area with a dozen people standing around. To Aspen, they were all new faces, but Charlie recognizes a few of them from alerts. Vex runs up immediately and hugs Oscar, thankful that he is safe. An older woman with greasy, shoulder length, gray hair walks up with a smile to embrace Jared.

"It's been too long Jared," the woman says as she hugs Jared. "Your mother would be proud."

"It's good to see you too, Elise," Jared responds.

"And this must be Aspen," Elise says as she turns to Aspen and holds Aspen's hands in hers. "My name is Elise, or just El; your choice. I'm so happy you're with us. You are beautiful."

"Elise; this us Charlie. He works at the NSA complex," Jared says as he points at Charlie

"Hello Charlie; none of this is possible without you. I thank you from the bottom of my heart," Elise says as she shakes hands with Charlie.

"Nice to meet you, Elise. I don't mean to rush, but we have an hour before I need to be back."

"I will do my best Charlie. Aspen... come with me."

Elise takes Aspen by the hand and brings her in front of everyone in the warehouse. A few stragglers come in late and everyone surrounds Aspen and Elise. Aspen looks around at all the worn out, tired faces of the men and women in the crowd. Some are carrying guns, some aren't. The clothes they are wearing are not the trend, not the newest fashion. Elise herself is wearing blue jeans with holes all over, with a black hoody that has seen better days.

Elise walks around the entire circle shaking hands and welcoming everyone before she joins back up with Aspen in the center.

"Welcome everyone. Thank you for coming. I know we rarely see each other like this, but we do need to be brief for safeties sake. With us tonight is Aspen James," Elise says as she acknowledges Aspen next to her. "No doubt you have heard her name over the airwaves the last week."

Elise sends Aspen back to Jared in the circle around Elise.

“Our good friend Jared was informed of a situation involving the robotic A.I. that we heard rumors about. It is all true. And Aspen is the key.”

Everyone around the room starts speaking to each other louder. They grow exponentially interested in what Elise has to say. Aspen has been under the impression that Jared was the commander of all the rebels. To her, it has become increasingly clear that Jared is simply a ranking man in an organized regime.

“These... A.I. are like us in every way. All the way down to the bones and the blood. They are spying machines that can watch, listen, and record everyone’s daily lives. But we have a solution. Once inside the Mimir, we will broadcast proof of the AFO’s treachery. We will send it all over America, Europe; everywhere. The world will know what the AFO is doing and they will be punished for it,” Elise says as she raises her voice at the end of her speech.

The room cheers at the speech by Elise.

“Now... I’m going to hand the floor to someone who helped make all of this possible,” Elise says before she looks at Charlie. “Everyone... this is Charlie, an AFO detractor who works at the NSA complex. Without him, we couldn’t have gotten Aspen. Without him, we couldn’t begin this operation. Without him... we couldn’t bring down the AFO. Charlie.”

Elise announces the introduction of Charlie to an applause. He walks out in front of everyone and starts to speak as Elise walks out of the circle and sits down.

After explaining the plan he has, in haste, Charlie throws a wrench in everyone's confidence.

"This needs to happen tomorrow. Sunday is a low staff day and it will be the easiest," Charlie says to whispers in the room.

"Why?" Elise asks.

"The director is growing suspicious of me. At some point I imagine his paranoia will kill me. Sunday is the best option and I won't live to the next one."

Elise locks eyes with Charlie for a moment before walking back into the circle.

"Then we will be ready," Elise says.

Once the plan is finalized, everyone disperses. Charlie is chomping at the bit to get back to the Sly Raccoon sooner than later. As everyone starts saying goodbye, Charlie grabs Jared on the shoulder.

"We need to go. Now."

÷

"Has anything changed with their locations yet?" Leadheim asks the analyst.

"No movement. Not even to the bathroom."

"How long has it been?"

"Um… around an hour forty since they both went into the restaurant."

Agent Leadheim is getting impatient. He waits in his car wondering suspiciously. He looks at the time and puts his binoculars down on the passenger seat. Leadheim gets out of his car in the rain, which has gotten heavier. He runs across the road to the opposing sidewalk and hops over a small drain. As he approaches the restaurant his heart starts beating in excitement to catch Charlie. When Leadheim is ten steps from the front window of the Sly Racoon, he hears the analyst in his ear.

"Their moving."

This cements Leadheim in place, making him to decide whether or not to continue forward or turn around.

"Agent Leadheim; both people have exited the Sly Raccoon. Clarissa is moving toward the back parking lot and Charlie is headed around back towards the front."

Leadheim, out of time, rushes forward and enters the front door of the restaurant. He sits down in the middle of two couples waiting to be seated.

"Clarissa is gone. Tracking the car now. Charlie has crossed the street and is in the parking garage."

"Let me know when he is gone so I can move."

"Charlie is gone. He is headed down the street. I found the car belonging to Carissa," the analyst says as Leadheim stands up and starts jogging to his car.

"Where's the car?" Leadheim asks as he gets in his car and starts the engine.

"Traveling down Larson Street. Car belongs to a Victoria Summers. Car must be stolen."

"Get the PD to pull the car over. I'm on the way."

Leadheim hits the gas on his car and heads a few blocks from the restaurant. He is informed by the analyst that the car is pulled over. When he is told of this, he can see the lights from the police car in the distance. He approaches the police car from behind and parks behind it. Leadheim gets out of his car and pulls up his badge so the officer can see that he is from the AFO. The officer approaches Leadheim near his cop car.

"Hello, Sir. Officer Hawkins," Hawkins says as he puts his hand out to shake, which Leadheim refutes.

"You can leave now," Leadheim says to Officer Hawkins.

"Here's her driver's license," Hawkins says as he hands Leadheim the driver's license.

Sure enough, the license is that of Victoria Summers, not Clarissa Jane like he was hoping. Leadheim walks over to the car and approaches the window. He leans down in and looks at the woman, who appears frightened and confused.

"Where's the phone?"

Victoria, and older woman, frantically reaches over to the passenger seat and grabs a phone that she hands to Leadheim.

“What happened? Who gave this to you?”

“A young girl gave it to me. Threatened to kill me if I didn’t drive away with it. She put a gun to my head.”

Agent Leadheim takes the phone and gives the license back to Victoria. He calls the analyst as he gets in his car.

“Yes, Sir.”

I need you to track down the real Clarissa Jane and track any vehicles that left the restaurant right before or after this one.”

“Understood, Sir.”

Agent Leadheim drives through the rain waiting on a call from the analyst. He is frustrated and determined. The traffic starts to slow down along with the city as the rain continues and businesses start to close their doors. A few miles later, Agent Leadheim receives a call from the analyst with a home address for Clarissa Jane. Leadheim starts to head toward the home address of Clarissa.

Once he arrives to the house in the outskirts of the city, Leadheim snatches the phone from the passenger seat and gets out. He slams the door behind him and starts walking up the concrete steps to an old yellow home. Leadheim rings the doorbell and waits until a woman opens the door.

Clarissa tells Agent Leadheim a similar story that Victoria told. Someone threatened her life and took her phone, telling her they would kill her family if she did not comply. Clarissa tells Leadheim they promised that she would get her phone back. Leadheim gives her the phone and walks away back down the concrete steps without saying a word. Once he gets inside his car, Leadheim grabs the steering wheel with both hands and starts screaming and moving in a bout of rage. He has been deceived and he is not handling it well.

He stops suddenly and looks up at the yellow house. Leadheim gets out quickly leaving the car door open. He jumps up the concrete steps and knocks rapidly on the door. Clarissa opens the door to surprise as Leadheim forces his way inside pushing her to the ground. She screams in terror as Leadheim tackles her and starts beating her face into the floor like he has mallets for hands. He takes out his rage on her until blood splatters up onto the wall. Clarissa lies dead on the floor with broken bones impacted into her head and a man twice her size kneeling over her.

Agent Leadheim sits up and looks at the body on the ground for a second before calling the analyst.

"Yes, Sir."

"Does Clarissa Jane have family?"

"Umm... she is divorced and has a daughter; Lilly Jane. Should live with her."

"I need a clean-up crew at her residence in twenty minutes. Two bodies."

Chapter 12

The morning comes quickly as Jared, Aspen, Oscar, and Vex walk out of the caves and hike towards the van. Everyone gets into the van and sits down with Oscar taking the wheel. The sun starts peeking through the clouds and glimmers through the branches of the forest as Oscar starts driving.

The van kicks up dirt and pine needles as they speed away toward the main road into the city. Aspen pays no mind to the bumps and stays focused on enacting her revenge for her family. She looks over at the body of Claudia that they moved to the van last night. It aggravates her even more.

All they have had to do now is steal a car in the city and get to the gates of the NSA complex around the same time Charlie does.

÷

With the curtains still drawn closed, Charlie finishes tying his tie on his favorite suit. He feels it appropriate being that today could be his last day. Charlie looks in the mirror and double checks his shave, plucking stragglers to look his best.

Once Charlie leaves the bathroom, he walks into his bedroom and pulls the curtains back allowing the light and viewing eyes inside. He looks in his kitchen cabinets and gazes at food sitting on the shelves, sighing as his appetite diminishes.

Charlie walks hard down the hallway, digging his heels in with every step. He hits the elevator button and watches the arrow above the door until a loud beep breaks his trance. The door opens for a mother and a small girl, who walk past Charlie in a hurry. He slips by and hits the star for the ground floor and begins to rapidly hit the close door key. He looks out the door and sees the small girl waving to him as the door shuts. The elevator stops a few more times on the way down, pushing Charlie to the back of the elevator.

The elevator reaches the ground floors, sending everyone pouring out every direction. Charlie slips through and glides his way past everyone he can as he rushes to the parking garage. As he brushes shoulders, he hears people remarking of his rudeness, but pays no mind. He only has one thing on his mind.

Once he gets to the garage, he gets in his car, shuts the door, and breaths. Charlie leans his head on his steering wheel and puts the key in the ignition. He grits his teeth as he turns the key and lets out a sigh of relief as the car starts with a slight hiccup and no explosion. Charlie sits up and quickly puts on his seat belt once he looks at the time. He puts his car into reverse and speeds out of the garage. Once he gets into the street, he puts his car in autonomous mode for the NSA complex.

A mile down the road, Charlie spots the white car that has been following him as of late. He looks at the time and sees that he will arrive to the complex a few minutes before the planned time.

÷

After catching up to Charlie and staying a safe distance away, Agent Leadheim reduces his speed and watches from afar. He grabs his phone and calls the analyst he has been working with.

"Yes Agent Leadheim."

"Have you found anything on vehicles leaving the restaurant last night?"

"I did. Every vehicle checked out except two. A black SUV at the time Stipper was there and a white SUV at the time he left. Both SUVs were reported stolen."

"What did you find?"

"Nothing yet. I'm still tracing them. They switched vehicles quite a bit."

"Figure it out. Quickly," Leadheim says before he hangs up the phone.

÷

After swapping vehicles at two different switch sites and hiding the van, Vex speeds up to make it to the NSA complex in time.

"Are we good?" Jared asks.

"We're good," Vex responds as she looks at the clock.

When they are a few miles from the complex, Vex spots Charlie's car and moves into position three car lengths behind him. Unknowingly, Vex places their car between Charlie and Agent Leadheim.

Charlie, busy keeping his eyes on his rear-view mirror, spots Vex in the traffic behind him and breathes a sigh of relief. The plan is in motion as the cars travel up into the mountains south of the city.

The exit for the NSA complex approaches quickly. Charlie exits followed by another car and then Vex, who rushes to get as close behind him as she can. Leadheim ends up two cars behind them. All the cars that exit from the highway drive up to one of the guards protecting the NSA. Vex is able to get right behind Charlie while Leadheim goes into a different lane.

"Cover yourselves," Vex whispers as they Jared and the others put blankets over themselves.

The car in front of Charlie gets waived through. The guard waves at Charlie to come forward.

"Good morning, Sir," the guard says.

"Code Forty-Six!" Charlie says quickly. "I need to get going!"

The guard motions to another man in security and they let Charlie drive away. Vex pulls up and uses the same code. Without hesitation, the guards allow Vex to drive through right behind Charlie.

Agent Leadheim sees Charlie and the other car drive right through security, which enrages him, causing him to honk his horn in protest. One of the guards immediately walks over as Leadheim gets out of his car.

"Why are they going in so quickly?" Leadheim yells out.

"It's an emergency, Sir. Get back in your vehicle."

"This is bullshit!" Leadheim yells out angrily.

The guard, visibly upset at Agent Leadheim and his choice of language, pulls out his gun and tells him to get back into his car. Leadheim, brewing with anger, gets back in his car after slamming the door. He starts to grind both his hands on the steering wheel, chafing the leather off the wheel and into his lap.

As Leadheim gets stuck at the gate, both Charlie and Vex arrive to the complex. Charlie drives into the main lot, closest to the utility building. Vex drives past and continues around the complex until she reaches the lot for the Mimir. She parks inconspicuously and waits for the next phase of the plan, laying backwards and out of sight.

Charlie pulls up near the sidewalk and puts his car in park. He gets out and grabs his suitcase, leaving his door open and car running. Charlie walks quickly across the courtyard toward the utility building. His plan is to disable the main power grid across the complex, disabling the security features on the walls around the entire complex. The only thing it does not disable is the Mimir, which has its own internal power.

Charlie slips his badge off his neck as he approaches the door to the building. He slides it through quickly and it denies him entry. Charlie breathes and slides it through slower. The door unlocks and beeps with a solid green light; allowing Charlie to pull the door open and slide inside.

Once he is in the utility building, Charlie walks quickly down a hallway surrounded by offices. He gets a feeling that everyone is watching him and can hear them talking amongst each other. Charlie is undeterred and keeps moving until he reaches the door that will bring him downstairs to the control rooms.

Charlie opens the door to the control room where several people are working diligently. Suddenly the alarms start blaring in the room. All the employees start looking at each other and at Charlie. Charlie looks around knowing that Leadheim got the alarms to go off. Knowing he is in a bind; Charlie pulls out his gun.

"Everybody get the fuck out!" Charlie screams as he fires several rounds into the ceiling.

The employees start running over each other to get to the door and outside. As they scramble, Charlie rushes to the main controls and lays down his suitcase. He inputs the code on his briefcase and opens it to retrieve the C4 he has stashed inside. Charlie takes the C4 carefully out of his briefcase and sets it up in the control room. After he gets the detonator ready, he stands up and walks towards the door, but hears people coming down the steps. He quickly locks the door and walks to the bomb.

He knows now that he will not escape the control room; and the control room will be his grave. As security starts banging on the door, tears start to roll down Charlie's face. They fire out the hinges and knob on the door before bursting in. Charlie chokes up and closes his eyes before pulling the trigger on the detonator.

÷

As soon as the alarms start blaring, Jared and his team start getting worried.

"What's going on Vex?" Jared asks muffled through the blanket.

"Alarms are going off, but the power is still on," Vex replies.

"Are we fucked?" Aspen asks.

"I don't know. Just hold on."

As they continue waiting for the power to shut off, a loud boom reaches their ears. They hear screaming and Vex starts to see smoke rising in the sky. The lights also go out.

"Was that the signal?" Aspen asks as Jared throws the blanket off himself.

"Yep. Let's move!" Vex screams out as she gets out of the car.

Jared reaches for the handle to the door to jump out. Oscar does the same on the other side, followed by Aspen. While Jared and Vex secure the area, Oscar goes into the trunk to carry Claudia.

Vex leads the way across the parking lot with an automatic rifle in her arms with Jared following closely behind. Oscar and Aspen take the rear as the group moves in almost perfect unison across the parking lot to the Mimir.

People are screaming and running across the complex as more explosions and gunfire erupt in the distance. The rest of ANA are attacking the walls surrounding the complex, led by Elise. All the turrets and alarm systems are now down due to the power failure, allowing easier access and preventing reinforcements from reaching the Mimir.

As the group approaches the Mimir, Vex and Jared fire upon a couple guards standing outside the doors. They shoot to disable the guards trying not kill them.

Jared and Vex rush up to the guards and put the barrels of their guns to the guards heads; Jared with one and Vex with the other. Oscar stays low nearby as Aspen keeps an eye out all around them.

"Which one of you mother fuckers is gonna cooperate?" Jared yells.

Both guards remain silent. As they look at each other.

"Figures," Vex says calmly as she fires a round through the guard's head.

Jared fires and kills the other guard as they start taking fire from behind them. Oscar starts firing with a pistol and yelling for them to get inside.

"Aspen! Grab an ID and get that door open!" Jared yells as he starts firing across the field and backing up to the doors.

Aspen gets down on her hands and knees and rips off the ID card from one of the guard's coats, which is covered in blood. She stands up and runs low to the door and starts sliding the ID through the scanner to get the door open. Once the scanner gives a green light, Aspen swings the door open and gets inside.

"Come on!" Aspen yells as everyone back up to the door and gets inside.

When everyone gets inside, they slowly back down the stairs toward the elevator waiting for someone to burst through the door.

"What do we do now?" Oscar asks.

"I'm thinking!" Jared yells.

In a tense moment of silence, the elevator beeps behind them prompting everyone to spin around quickly. The door opens and people begin pouring out until they see the guns pointed at them as they put their hands up.

"This solves our problem," Vex says.

"Yes, it does... Vex, cover the door," Jared says to Vex as he addresses the people on the elevator. "Listen up! I need to go down and only need one of you. The rest can leave."

There is silence as no one volunteers.

Jared swings his rifle over his shoulder and pulls out his pistol as he grabs a young woman by the hair and puts the gun to her head in front of the elevator.

"I will kill her. I don't care. I don't give a shit. Who is going down?" Jared yells out.

The room remains silent without a volunteer, but with gasps from the group in the elevator. Jared pulls the trigger and kills the woman to screams. Jared grabs a guy from the elevator and puts the gun up to his head, asking again for volunteers. When no one steps forward, Jared shoots and kills the man.

"Jared!" Aspen yells at the top of her lungs. "Stop!"

Aspen walks in front of Jared before he grabs another person from the elevator. She looks at all the faces in the elevator. Some are crying, some are afraid, and some have zero emotion.

"You all know me. You all know who I am. I used to be you. Until you murdered my husband! My children!" Aspen yells as she starts to cry. "A revolution is coming. Who is brave enough to stand up to the tyranny!"

The door up above swings open and gunshots ring out as Vex start firing.

"Hurry up!" yells Vex.

"Who is brave enough?" Aspen asks over the gunfire.

Jared jumps up in front of Aspen, but Aspen stops him and sends him back.

"Who is brave enough," Aspen says through tears.

Suddenly a short man from the back of the elevator raises his hand and steps forward with his hands raised. As he steps out of the elevator, people start calling him a traitor and spitting at him. Jared yells at the crowd to get off the elevator and fires into the air. Oscar and Vex hop down the stairs and join the rest of the group in the elevator as the people rush up the stairs to the door.

"What's your name?" Aspen asks as she grabs his shaking hands.

"Taylor... Taylor Draff."

"Thank you, Taylor," Aspen says as she gives him a hug.

"Let's go!" yells Jared.

As Taylor puts in his ID; he inputs in his pass code and speaks his name. The doors to the elevator start to close. The people from the elevator reach the door to exit the Mimir and are shot and killed as they try to leave. The doors shut and the elevator starts moving down. Taylor becomes visibly shaken as he sees his coworkers mowed down by machine gun fire. He begins shaking tremendously and grinding his teeth. Vex notices this and steps in front of him.

"Taylor right," Vex says as she grabs Taylor's shoulders, propping him up.

"Yeah."

"You did the right thing. You are a survivor. Please help us."

"Ok. Ok."

"Good. Once we get down there, I need your help setting up the emergency broadcast system. Do you know how to do that?"

"Yeah. We all do."

"Good. You are amongst friends now."

Taylor agrees to help Vex right before the elevator beeps that it has reached the bottom. As the doors start to open, hands start reaching into the elevator trying to get in. When they open enough to see guns in their faces the employees back up with their hands up.

"Back the fuck up!" Jared says as he takes the lead on exiting the elevator.

The group shifts to one side of the hallway with their fingers on the triggers while the employees move on the other side. They shift slowly until people start piling onto the elevator away from Jared and the rest of the group. Jared takes the lead into the empty control room with the rest of the group in tow. After it is secured, Jared turns around and lowers his weapon.

"Lets do this," Jared says.

Everyone nods in agreement.

"Alright. Oscar, Vex; you guys work with and protect uh... Taylor and get the EBS up and running. Aspen; you and me are going to pay a visit to the director."

The team breaks apart as Aspen and Jared take off toward the offices upstairs to confront Director Harlow. Vex, Oscar, and Taylor start running towards the front of the control room to engage the Emergency Broadcast System.

Taylor gets onto the computer that controls the EBS while Vex keeps an eye out. Oscar places Claudia into the seat next to Taylor who looks uneasy after he looks at her.

"How long is this going to take?" Oscar asks as he pulls out a pistol.

"Umm... Thirty minutes. Hopefully."

As Taylor types away on the keyboard, Vex keeps an eye on the elevator. The door opens and Leadheim steps out and is immediately fired upon by Vex. Leadheim ducks and jumps behind a wall before beginning to shoot back. Vex and Oscar quickly jump behind some desks for cover while Taylor simply brings his head and shoulders down closer to the monitor.

"Better make that thirty minutes faster!" Vex yells out as she fires her rifle.

Vex and Oscar exchange gunshots with Leadheim as they move up in the control room towards the elevator. One gives covering fire while the other moves. They move back and forth until they are fifty feet from the elevator.

"I won't kill you if you give up you fuckhead. Just throw your gun out and no one has to die."

"I thought you were the AFO. I'm with the ANA," Leadheim yells out. "I'm coming out, please don't shoot."

Leadheim throws his gun out into the hallway so Vex and Oscar can see it. He stands up slowly and steps into the middle of the hallway with his hands up.

"We are on the same side," Leadheim says as he walks toward them.

Agent Leadheim continues speaking of friendship as he walks toward Vex. With an extra pistol tucked into his back and out of view, he hopes to catch them by surprise. Once Leadheim gets within twenty feet of them, Vex fires her gun into his legs, sending Leadheim falling to the ground screaming. Vex stands up and immediately runs up to Leadheim, who is screaming in agony.

"What they fuck are you doing Vex!" Oscar yells as Vex stands over top of Leadheim.

"We're ANA. Not the ANA you hole," Vex says as she unloads her gun into Leadheim's head. "Let's get that broadcast up. Watch the door," Vex says to Oscar as she walks to the front of the control room.

÷

While Vex, Oscar, and Taylor work to get the Emergency Broadcast System going; Jared and Aspen head upstairs to visit with Director Thomas Harlow. They reach the door to his office, indicated by a placard on the wall. Jared takes a deep breath and has Aspen open the door. She flings it open quickly as Jared rushes in first with his rifle followed closely by Aspen with a pistol.

They go into the office expecting possible resistance from Harlow, but there is none. Harlow is sitting behind his desk drinking liquor from a cup with melting ice, swishing it around. He is drunk and leaning back in his chair.

“Welcome. To the AFO,” Harlow says as he raises his glass. “Cheers.”

Harlow slams his drink and stands up from his chair, prompting Jared and Aspen to both clutch their weapons. He puts up both his hands to show he doesn’t have a gun as he walks over to make another drink.

“You guys look tense. Do you want a drink?”

“Why the fuck are you so calm?” Jared asks.

“Well… I don’t have much time left,” Harlow says as he falls back into his chair. “And our plans worked to perfection.

“What plans?” Jared asks.

“Getting you here. In this building. With her,” Harlow says as he points at Aspen.

“What do you mean?” Jared asks intently.

“That woman right there is Claudia with Aspen’s mind. We switched you at the club. You probably woke up a little bit sluggish. I knew Charlie was the mole. I knew he would reach out to you guys after he saw that ‘Aspen’ worked at the library that you guys needed to break into. The only hiccup was when you hit your head in the car accident. It busted your control chip. So… we had to adjust a few things, but we made it happen.”

Jared and Aspen are taken aback.

“That’s not true,” Aspen says.

“It is. Think about it. Think about everything,” Harlow says. “Jared... did you really think it would be this easy?”

With Jared and Aspen still processing what Director Harlow said, he reaches toward his desk.

“Don’t move mother fucker!” Jared yells.

“Relax,” Harlow says as he pulls a knife from his top drawer. “I’m not going to kill you.”

Director Harlow begins to twirl the knife on his desk. It is solid black handle with a fine steel blade with a slight curve.

“Do you recognize this blade, Jared?”

Jared puts one hand over the scar on his face.

“Yep. This blade gave you your scar,” Harlow says before he slides it across the desk. “I want you to have it, Jared.”

Without warning, Jared fires a single round into Director Harlow’s head. Blood splatters on Harlow’s chair and the curtains behind him. Jared looks at Harlow’s lifeless body for a second before he turns and sees the knife still sitting on the desk. He reaches out and holds it in his hand.

“What the fuck is going on!” Aspen yells out grabbing her head.

Jared walks over to Aspen and embraces her.

"We'll figure this out. Lets keep this between ourselves for now. Lets go."

Jared and Aspen leave Harlow dead in his chair as they leave the office and head downstairs to group up with everyone else. They pass by Leadheim on their way to the front of the control room.

"What happened here?" Jared asks in regards to Leadheim.

"Just a minor inconvenience," Vex responds.

"Do you have the EBS ready to go Taylor?" Aspen asks.

"Just a few more clicks; and... you're ready to go."

The screen in the front of the control room turns on and loads into the EBS program. The screens on the sides of the main screen start loading as well. Vex and Oscar have Claudia set up in front of the camera on a chair sitting up so the world can see her face. Jared stands up in front of her and waits for the EBS to load up. Everyone is excited to finally take down the AFO and expose the Judas Project to the world.

Aspen looks at Claudia wondering if Director Harlow is telling the truth. Is the dead body propped up on the chair the real Aspen... or is she.

The program loads on the screen triggering the camera to turn on. Jared begins to speak, but then the power suddenly cuts out. Everything goes black and panic and frustration begin to set in. Jared looks around and starts questioning what's going on, until the main screen turns on with a shadowed figure sitting front and center.

"Did you really think you could win?" the voice says. "You are not as smart as I would expect my own flesh and blood to be. You are going to unite the country more than ever before."

"How do you figure?" yells Jared.

Tarrick laughs. "You are thinking so small. You see; I'm not going to send anyone or anything to stop you. You attacked the NSA and killed hundreds, maybe thousands of people. You think you orchestrated the perfect plan... but in reality; you were played."

"Everyone will wake up from your bullshit one day and we will kill you!" yells Aspen.

"I will kill you myself," Jared yells as he raises his rifle.

"I look forward to it... son."

Jared screams and unloads his rifle into the screen, shattering it into millions of pieces. He begins to cry and falls down to the ground with his hands over his face. Aspen goes down onto the ground and holds Jared and comforts him. Everyone else gathers around.

"We need to get out of here," Oscar says.

"Oscar's right," Jared says as he wipes his face and stands up with Aspen. "We need to go."

“Not yet,” Aspen says as she grabs the knife out of Jared’s pocket.

“What are you doing?” Jared asks in a concerned voice.

“No sympathy; only revolution,” Aspen says before she takes the knife and slices her cheek. “Fuck the AFO.”

They leave the Mimir defeated with more questions than answers.

Epilogue

Don't believe what they tell you

.

.

"If you are just tuning in with us on Channel 5 news, the NSA complex was attacked today…"

"Terrorists killed thousands of innocent, hard-working citizens…"

"Senior AFO leader and Director of the NSA, Thomas Harlow was found executed by the barbarians…"

"The ANA is claiming responsibility for the attack."

"No one is safe until the ANA is killed for their treason to the Free States."

"President Welch vows revenge and orders full military action against the terrorists…"

"Polls show 100 percent support behind the AFO…"

"Polls show 100 percent support for President Welch and his decision to root out the ANA with deadly force…"

"Polls show 100 percent support…"

"100 percent support for the AFO…"

"100 percent support…"

"100 percent."

www.ingramcontent.com/pod-product-compliance
Lightning Source LLC
LaVergne TN
LVHW010545160826
845677LV00013B/3009

9798362623500